Praise for Nuke Jersey

"The author's sense of humor (........................... s I read a sentence and wondered .... me of the ideas. I laughed often t .... ery easy to suspend disbelief, ever .... bit of everything in this book, politic............................... sm, WMDs, science, social issues, NJ mob families, military . . . and zombies, er . . . "the infected." It's almost like I can take every major movie/TV series growing up and put them all together, add zombies and creative writing skills and you get this series, making the series feel familiar and comforting, while still very fresh/new (which sounds impossible, but Neil Cohen did it)." *–Dr. Terry Oroszi, Assistant Professor, Molecular Geneticist, Terrorist Researcher, CBRN Defense Director, and Strategic Planner*

"Neil Cohen's book is a must read. As a survivor of ten military deployments and hurrican Katrina, I must say that I couldn't put this book down. Those who love the end of the world type genre will love this book." *–Larry C. James, Colonel (retired) U.S. Army and Professor, School of Professional Psychology, Wright State University*

"An interesting method of kicking off the zombie apocalypse that leads to an interesting twist in zombie anatomy." *–DreadCentral.com*

"Details long missing from zombie lore are sure to please the zombie fan who wants answers." *–Zom-B.com*

"One of the best books I've read in a while in regards to the zombie apocalypse. This is a total different take from your usual zombies biting and infecting people." *–Anna Olvera, CREATORS.CO*

"I can readily admit that Exit Zero has frightened me to the very core. Until now I've been a massive zombie fan and enjoyed the movies, books and TV shows for what they are; fiction. This book is disturbing because it demonstrates the ease of how a massive pandemic could be engineered and controlled by any number of large corporations, terrorist cells, or even our own governments." *–ZWeapons.com*

"Neil Cohen is a tireless advocate, working to keep the zombie genre undead." *–Robin Justice, WalkerStalkerCon*

Also by Neil A. Cohen

Exit Zero

Pope Judas of Jersey

NUKE Jersey

NEIL A. COHEN

A PERMUTED PRESS BOOK
ISBN: 978-1-61868-741-8
ISBN (eBook): 978-1-61868-740-1

Nuke Jersey:
© 2017 by Neil A. Cohen
All Rights Reserved

Cover art by Christian Bentulan

PERMUTED
PRESS

Permuted Press, LLC
permutedpress.com

Published in the United States of America

CONTENTS

AUTHOR'S NOTE

The final time I recall the majority of my childhood friends together in one place was the early 1990s. The location was a beach house on the Jersey Shore. The wooden structure—overlooking a small, poorly maintained beachfront—was owned by one of the brothers I loosely based the characters known as the Sullivans, also known as The Mutants. I know it sounds like a clichéd, douchebag thing to say, but it really was a different time. There was none of the PC bullshit that exists today. The nonsense we got away with back then would have gotten us expelled from school, locked up, and sent off to sensitivity re-education camp today. I am not saying this is a good thing or a bad thing, it just was what it was.

It was an era when Senator Patrick Moynihan was lamenting that our country was defining deviancy down—what was once considered abnormal was now normal—but we, my friends and I, were attempting to raise deviancy up to an all new level.

It was a time when porn could only be found hidden in your dad's closet, not in his browser history.

There were no Twitter, Facebook, Instagram or other social media platforms to publicly document the debauchery.

And with no evidence came no consequences. No consequences meant no inhibitions.

There was freedom to screw up.

No harm, no foul.

No victim, no crime.

No blood... Well, there was blood.

It was the last weekend of the first summer post high school, yet there was not the feeling of melancholy most would experience at this time in one's life. The core group had been together since they were allowed to play outside. Segregation only really began in grade school, where you were sent off to Catholic school or public school. Each had their pros and cons. Catholic school meant you had a good shot at college and a future. Public school was mainly a place to kill time for four years till you began your union trade or married your first ex-wife.

Those parents with the financial resources usually chose the private school route. My parents had the resources, they just did not give a shit, so I was dumped in public school, which is why you may catch a misspelling or five in this book.

Now, just because you were lucky enough to get into the private school did not mean you were guaranteed to graduate from that same institution. God gave man free will, and many of my friends used that free will to fuck things up so bad that God kicked their asses to the curb, and thus, they ended up slumming it with the rest of us in public school.

Yet the core group of my friends all remained close, those in public school and those in Catholic school.

While individuals had drifted in and out of the group over the years—sometimes leaving for extended periods of time—there was no permanently escaping the orbit, for the gravity of the group compelled each of us back into the fold, whether we wanted to be there or not.

By the time that final summer ended, there had already been a novel's worth of nonsense. A story that will be written one day, once all the statutes of limitation have expired, and we are too old to care what our coworkers and children think of us. No one will ever look at us the same way once all of the tales are told. Sure, all kids have their growing up war stories of drinking beer in the woods, being chased by cops, and the inevitable, usually regrettable, loss of virginity. But again, I will pull the douchebag card and state for the record that our stories were different. Someday I may tell those stories, but not now.

There is no real reason to share these tales. There are no lessons to be learned from reading about the events. We learned nothing from experiencing them.

We did not know at the time it would be our final gathering. We assumed weddings and reunions were sure to follow, occasions where we would once again congeal. But it was never again to be. Something changed during those final days together, something subtle, invisible, yet powerful enough to fracture the bonds that were holing us together.

It is analogous to a slow drip from a toilet tank above your dining room ceiling. Drip by drip, the water permeates the layers of drywall, weakens the fabric, and loosens the seams. A slow, silent, hidden leak. Each drip adds to the stagnant puddle. Drip by drip, until the structure can take no more and the ceiling collapses down onto a perfectly set dining table below. This is followed by a wave of putrid brown water that forever stains everything it touches.

A similar such leak must have been growing inside us. For how long, nobody can say, and the amount of time this slow drip had been occurring was different for each of us.

What that *drip drip drip* was building to was a final cymbal-crash crescendo of a party that took place on that final gathering on that final weekend together.

If those walls could talk, they would puke.

And later scream in agony as the entire house burned to the ground, forever erasing the location of the events that took place within from this earth—but not our memories.

It was that weekend when I first realized Exit Zero was real. While I cannot yet reveal the true events of those days, as many involved are now moms and dads, bosses and employees, doctors, lawyers, and craftsmen, all of whom require some degree of anonymity and plausible deniability, I still knew these were real characters that were ripe for the page. I wanted to tell their stories, to share these characters, these friends of mine. And I wanted to have them fight zombies.

INTRODUCTION

Your life's story is just that: a story.

Horror, fantasy, comedy or love story.

You won't know till it's over which one it is. And don't bother trying to write it all out ahead of time, because like most life stories, there is no real set plot line, no theme, no universal truth or divine plan.

Your life's story will be nothing more than just a bunch of random shit that happens.

So don't worry if someone else's life seems more important than yours. More planned out, more thought through, luckier than yours.

It's not.

Their life's story is as random as yours. So just enjoy the story of *your* life as it unfolds.

Don't nitpick, don't criticize, don't search for a plot or structure, and don't get hung up on typos, misspellings, grammar, tensing, or punctuation errors in your life's story.

Just relax, have fun, and enjoy the fucking story.

1

ERNIE

Ernie adjusted himself in the driver's seat of the PCRC Containment truck as the morning sun flirted with the horizon. He shifted back and forth to ensure his butt felt right in the groove, fixed the side mirror, and reached down to do a quick ball adjustment before his ride-along passenger arrived.

He had been driving an infected containment route for about two weeks and this would be his third ride-along candidate. He knew the other two weren't going to return. This job was not for everyone. Really should *not* be for anyone, but times being what they were, he felt he was a necessary part of the solution.

He looked in the rear view mirror and saw today's guest walking up. A young woman. *This is going to be different,* he thought. The last two were men. Well, college boys, but close to being men.

Since the PCRC had closed all the universities in the state for the purposes of setting up quarantine zones, the displaced students were eager to find any work they could until they were allowed to leave Jersey.

As the blonde-haired twenty something made her way up to the cab and climbed up into the passenger side, Ernie wished he had dressed a little spiffier today. Could you blame him? She was more than a little attractive. He also hoped she held her puke till she was outside the cab, unlike two of the previous so-called men he had tried to train.

"Hello," she said. "My name is Juniper. I guess you'll be my tour guide through the Jersey Apocalypse today." Her demeanor was bright and bubbly.

She's not going to last past the first containment stop, Ernie thought.

"Yes, ma'am" he replied. "I guess I am. My name's Ernie and *technically* I'm one of the more seasoned professionals at this here brand new occupation. It's my ninth day on the job." He smiled. "You, young lady, are learning from an old pro."

"Am I your first trainee?

"No, ma'am, you're not. You're my third. But you are the first of the female persuasion."

"Well, I'm glad I'm in good hands," she replied with a grin to match Ernie's.

He started up the truck and drove out of the secure perimeter surrounding the university that used to be Juniper's school and was currently a Skell quarantine zone.

She said, "So, how did you get this job?"

"Call it fate, but the previous jobs I held afforded me the opportunity to attain the skill set that makes this a perfect fit. I am uniquely qualified for this profession. The stars certainly did align."

Juniper said, "What former jobs?"

"Well, you see, my father was a professional man. A man of higher education—a doctor. But he did not see the educational path as being right for me. As I recall, he told me that college was not for everyone, and I was not all that bright, and that he was going to flush money down the toilet sending me to college.

"So, after high school, I went into waste management. I was a garbage man, to use less politically correct terminology. Later, I drove the recycling route. I enjoyed that job more. Felt like I was helping the environment.

"I did that for some years."

Juniper wrinkled her nose. "Your father sounds awful!"

"Aw, he wasn't that bad. He was just an unhappy man. I really don't think he wanted a child, but as you should know better than me—women usually get what they want. Later on in life, my father became what I used to call 'the most feared man in Newark prison.'"

Juniper looked over at him with a raised eyebrow.

Ernie gave her a sly smile. "He had gone to work for the state and became the Northern State Prison dentist in Newark. He then landed me a job as a prison guard. Or, as we were referred to, prison officers. But we were guards none the less. We moved men from one location to another. We restrained men. We kept men from hurting themselves and others.

"So you can say, between the recycling route and the prison gig, I attained all the skills I needed for this particular endeavor." Ernie looked over to Juniper as the truck cab bounced on cracked asphalt. "What about you, young lady, what was your course of study before all this ugliness befell our fair state?"

"Cultural anthropology."

"Oh, Lord. That was an academic pursuit my father would *definitely* have considered flushing money down the toilet. I hope you do well today, as this may be the best paying gig you'll ever land."

They drove through the nearly empty streets and arrived at the first stop.

They saw some of the Kraken Systems that had been deployed around New Jersey—sound machines that emitted a low-level hum to draw the infected towards them like moths to a flame. The Krakens then kept the Skells calm and docile, rather than the ravenous, flesh-seeking missiles they usually were.

There weren't any monsters around the first Kraken site.

"Humpf," Ernie said, confused and a bit disappointed. He stood there for a moment, looking around the immediate area to ensure no stragglers were on their way. "Okay, no pickups. On to stop two." He started up the truck again and began driving.

Juniper kept the conversation going with more questions. "I already asked how you fell into this job, but do you *like* it?"

"It's not so bad. I get to meet new people, like you. I spend most of the day outdoors, not in some gray cube like an office drone. Not behind prison walls. Independent. And, again, I feel like I'm helping people."

She nodded. Her eyes bobbed from the view out the front windshield to the side window. "What exactly are we doing here anyway? How are we supposed to contain and collect if there's nothing to...contain and collect?"

"This job entails enduring a lot of boredom followed by periods of absolutely pants shitting terror, if you'll excuse my French. You see, if they are close enough to the hum from those Kraken boxes they got all around the state, then these things are as calm as can be. They are totally spaced out, like on opium. That sound is their opiate. The opiate of the masses. The infected just stand there and we gather them up, hustle them into the back of the trucks, and off we go." Ernie shrugged, like it was no big deal. "But the ones we see that are *not* around the boxes, those mothers are dangerous. They're fast, vicious, and fearless. We don't go near them. We report them to the PCRC headquarters and the contractors come clean up."

Juniper wriggled in her seat, trying to get comfortable the same way Ernie had before.

He continued. "Not sure if you noticed, but not all Skells are the same. Some people weather the infection better than others. They don't become so emaciated. From what I hear, if someone was a real tub o' lard before they got infected, like a real pachyderm fatso, the infection kind of pauses, or stops completely. Leaving them not like a walking skeleton like the others, but more like one of those marathon runners. Still skinny, athletic skinny. Not *healthy* athletic looking, but 'someone who exercises way too much' type skinny. Those ones can be feisty. Those ones, headquarters wants to know about immediately when we pick up."

Juniper nodded again. Seemed like she understood, but Ernie knew that even college kids who were supposed to be smart had a way of half-heartedly agreeing while being lost in their own brains. Still, this girl seemed like she might be made of harder stuff.

So he tried to keep her attention with conversation. "One time in the prison, I had this marathon runner as an inmate. He was a lawyer who was involved in some sort of financial scam. This lawyer sued the prison, claiming that since he was a marathon runner and running was like his religion, he should be allowed to run every day. They were inhibiting his religious worship by not allowing him to run. The lawyer won and so this guy got to go running in the courtyard every day as his quote, unquote, *worship time*." Ernie looked over to Juniper, but she was still staring out the window. He gripped the wheel and kept on. "Well anyway, this marathon guy looked awful to me. He was fit, but not in healthy shape. All bone, lean muscle and veins. Not sure what that was all about. Why would you *want* to look like that? Kept talking about resting heart rate and shit, but to me, I thought he was just running himself to death.

"About a year later, this guy gets some sort of foot issue. The doctor tells him to stop running. He says no, cut my foot off. No shit, this asshole sued the state *again* for the surgery and won so that he can have his right foot cut off and this flat plastic prosthesis blade attached so he could keep running. Who the fuck cuts off his own foot, makes himself a cripple, just so he can keep running? So every day, this guy goes out to the yard, has the prosthesis attached, runs in circles for a couple hours, and then turns the foot back in. Real fanatic."

Juniper mumbled in agreement. "Mmhmm."

Ernie said, "Well, I think of that guy when I see some of these sturdier Skells. Headquarters has a lot more interest in those than others. When we pick up one of those physically fit Skells, we notify the drop off point ahead of time, and those Skells get taken elsewhere."

That seemed to get her attention back. "Where are they taken?"

"Hell if I know. Supposedly, they're housed away till a cure can be found, but I don't see any doctors around the quarantine zones. Lots of contractors, lots of guns, and those intake buildings they set up. I hear, though, just idle gossip, mind you, and you did not hear this from me, but I hear they're being trained."

"Trained?"

"Yeppers. That is what I hear. A drunken contractor was shooting his mouth off at the bar one night. Something about a boot camp for special Skells. He called them Vinny's or something like that"

"Boot camp? Like a military boot camp?"

Ernie shrugged a little. "Just what I heard."

They sat in silence while Ernie weaved his way to the second pick up point. As they pulled up, they could see this one had attracted Skells. It had also attracted taggers. Someone had spray-painted on the side of the Kraken unit: "Must Gut Them."

"Weird stuff," Ernie said.

"What?"

"Jogging as a religion."

Juniper cocked an eye. Made a noise like, "Mrm." That sort of noise that was a cross between "I agree" and "Go fuck yourself, I'm thinking bigger."

Ernie brought the truck to a standstill about fifteen feet from the Kraken. He jumped out of the cab and turned to his passenger. "Little lady, you can watch through the windshield if you prefer, just to get eyes on the process. No need to jump right in with both feet."

She opened her door and jumped down, landing solidly on both her feet. "Like that?" she asked.

Ernie smiled. "Let's see how long this bravado will last."

He opened a panel on the truck, one underneath the large PCRC Containment Team logo painted across the side. He pulled out his two tools for wrangling Skells. "Here's the fishing equipment." He said to Juniper, putting the two long poles over his shoulder. One appeared to be little more than a reinforced pool skimmer, only the skimmer mesh was loose like a butterfly net. The other was a shorter pole that could extend and retract with the push of a button.

He walked over to the first male Skell. The man was a new infection, not fully turned. He plopped the net over the man's head and then pressed the button that telescoped the other pole, which had a collar-like clamp that extended from the end. He placed the open clamp at the base of the man's neck and a sensor on the back of the clamp detected the obstruction and snapped shut around the man's throat. It locked tight.

"It reminds me of a Venus Flytrap that I had when I was a kid," Juniper said.

Ernie walked the infected man into the back of the truck. It was sectioned into four cattle shoots.

Juniper walked to the rear of the truck to watch how Ernie stored the Skell for safe transport and she noticed the Kraken hum was replicated in the back of the vehicle. Four speakers up on each corner played the sound, ensuring the infected would remain docile once separated from the Kraken.

Ernie navigated the man down the first shoot, using the pool skimmer to guide the infected. He placed the male Skell up against the wall, released the neck clamp with his right hand, pushed the man backwards against the wall using the pool skimmer in his left, and a wall-mounted clamp with its own sensor locked around the man's neck, holding him firm.

She noticed how the wall-mounted clamps could be adjusted up and down, depending on the height of the infected that was being contained. She also noticed that in the second cattle shoot row, the neck clamps were all no higher than four feet off the ground.

That must be where the children were contained.

Ernie already had a second man clamped and was attaching him to the wall next to the first. "How about I leave the female up to you?"

"Now, Ernie, that sounds a little sexist. You don't think I could have contained the men?"

"I do apologize, young lady, no offense intended," he said, removing his ball cap and taking a deep bow as if he were a southern gentlemen meeting Scarlett O'Hara.

She took hold of the two poles and marched toward her prey. The woman was in pretty awful shape. She had been infected for some time. Her skin resembled leather wrapped around bone. The stomach protruded.

Juniper said, "Why do their stomachs swell like that? Acid or bloating?"

"Damned if I know, but I sure hope none of them burst. I tell you, that would have me losing my lunch."

She gently placed the netting over the woman's head. The bedraggled female Skell spun her head around and she snapped her jaws at Juniper, who jumped a little, but kept her grip on the pole.

"They do that sometimes," Ernie said. "You need to get that neck clamp on her lickity split."

Juniper placed the clamp up against the woman's neck and it sealed shut. She saw then that between the woman's teeth were strips of flesh and tendon.

Juniper felt the bile rise up, but was able to control it. She got a whiff of the woman. The Skell did not smell like a corpse should. Juniper had been around fresh corpses when she went to a crime reenactment farm for a term paper. It was an FBI area that used actual corpses in differing states of decay to so that pathologists could learn the sequential states of decay.

This woman smelled more like rancid ground beef. Like the time her mother had bought a pound of fresh hamburger and forgot it in the car over a summer weekend. The stink was distinctive.

She maneuvered the ragged woman into the back of the truck and down the aisle the first two men were housed. She put the female Skell up against the wall. The woman started to jerk violently. She shoved the woman against the sensor and the clamp closed around her neck. The woman kept flailing, even though the two men remained calm from the humming sound.

Juniper lifted the skimmer off the female Skell's head and rushed toward the back of the truck. The woman moved up and down like a piston, slamming her jaw into the metal clamp before shooting back up again. Each time the woman's head came down, smashing her lower jaw on the clamp, it ravaged her skull and shattered her teeth. She made one last violent push up and pull down, and her head popped off her neck like a thumb popping off the yellow flower of a dandelion. The head hit the wooden slats on the floor and rolled in a circle. The body fell to its knees and then stood up. The body then ran in the direction of Juniper, unstable and bouncing off either side of the cattle shoot, but scrambling with purpose.

Juniper screamed and even Ernie let out a horrified yelp. Juniper dove from the back of the truck and was caught by Ernie. The two tumbled to the ground.

The headless woman kept on her manic race, leaving her rolling dead cranium behind. The body reached the back of the truck and slammed to the ground. It awkwardly made its way back to its feet and bolted down the road, weaving as if it were dizzy. Dizzy and headless.

They watched in silence as the body charged down the empty street.

Juniper panted. "Has that happened before?" She found her feet and secured them against the cracked asphalt.

Ernie shook his head. "No, I can truly say it has not."

"Do we...go get her?"

"Fuck no. She's got no head, I couldn't secure her if I wanted to."

They both stood in silence for a few minutes.

Ernie said, "Young lady, would you like me to take you back to the HQ?"

"No," she said. She balled her fists at her sides as sweat poured down her cheeks. Breathed through her nose. "I really want to know what the hell just happened."

2
So WHAT THE HELL HAPPENED?

The zombie apocalypse had begun in New Jersey. While unexpected, no one was really all that surprised. After all, where else better than in the state that America loves to hate?

The Skell virus had been an unintended consequence of research meant to help mankind. The road to Skell was paved with good intentions. The concept was proposed by Dr. Woodrow Coleman, who wanted to grow A-grade meat in a lab via cattle stem cells. Inexpensive, healthy, protein created without the need for raising and slaughtering growth hormone-injected livestock. It would satisfy the animal rights activists, the anti-GMO crowd, the carbon footprint reduction crowd, and the meat for dinner crowd.

It could change the planet, if it only worked.

But it didn't.

This failure did not stop the largest defense contractor in the country, the Post Conflict Restoration Corporation (PCRC) from taking on the challenge, and lucrative contracts, to make it so.

After all, the President of the United States had already announced the Affordable Meals Act, which would provide this low cost, eco-friendly meat to "food deserts" around the country. Maxwell Gold, the president of PCRC, had never met a challenge he could not conquer. For decades, he had served powerful men, ensuring that the president received whatever he desired; be it a position of importance to satisfy, and distract, an ambitious first lady, or the removal of a troublesome Supreme Court Justice through "natural causes." Maxwell was the man with the plan.

The PCRC had been approached by the current president, as well as representatives from the Congress and Senate, to put in place a plan that would allow current elected officials to remain in office indefinitely, and for the American public to accept a new form of "democracy" that no longer involved voting.

Maxwell's plan was simple. First was to instill a sense of urgency into the public, a crisis so overwhelming that everyone would turn to the federal government to save and protect them.

Second, he needed to spread a different kind of mindset throughout the country. To infuse the population with the type of people who would be more than comfortable living under dictatorship. A populace that would be so appreciative of what they had, what had been given to them by the government, that they would see no reason for change or dissent.

The third part of the plan he did not share with anyone other than his closest inner circle. The president and congressional representatives and senators would indeed get what they wanted: an absolute, unchallenged ruling class. Unfortunately, none of them would live to benefit from this new arrangement.

The president chose a live televised address to the nation, where he would explain that the new Skell pandemic was a severe threat facing America, and that extreme executive actions were needed to ensure the safety of the American public and stability of the nation. He was to demonstrate that the entirety of the United States government was in agreement on these actions, and to prove this bipartisanship, officials from all three branches of government would be in the chamber with him to listen to his speech and stand and applaud in unity. But, just prior to this historic, unprecedented speech, they gathered to enjoy a sumptuous dinner, with a main course of steak provided by the PCRC.

Maxwell had enacted phase three.

The nation watched as the effects of that meal kicked in midway through the live telecast. Congressmen began eating senators. Senators were eating cabinet members. Supreme Court Justices ate the Joint Chiefs of Staff and the president ate his VP. By the time the Capitol Police were able to break down the doors of the sealed room, there was no one left to save. They were all dead or dying. That is, except for the sole elected official who was not in attendance. A young, freshman congressman from New Jersey named Patrick Callahan.

For the residents of New Jersey, the carnage was not just on the television. Soon it was on the parkway, on the turnpike, in their back yards, and in their bedrooms.

Skells did not bring about the immediate societal collapse one would expect. The government did not cease functioning, business and commerce continued, and people moved on with their lives—it's just that now it was a life rife with monsters.

The people of New Jersey first reacted, and then adapted, to life among the infected, or Skells as they had been named, due to their skeletal appearance. Skells were not re-animated corpses, they were simply infected individuals who had an insatiable addiction to human flesh. An addiction brought about either by their own consumption of the Modified Embolic Animal Tissue or M.E.A.T., which they believed to be lab-created beef grown from animal stem cells. Unbeknownst to the consumer, MEAT had been created out of human stem cells.

The Skell virus was also transmitted through contact with the infected. Those bitten, but who managed to escape before being entirely consumed, also became Skells. The amount of time it took infection to overtake a person depended upon their body mass. The more body fat, the longer it took the virus to burn through and melt the humanity away. Those that were morbidly obese even had the potential to survive the infection if it burned itself out before the wasting away was complete. For once, survival was not meant for the fittest.

That was two weeks ago, but people were already accepting the new normal. Life with Skells meant new rules and regulations, new bureaucracy, and new authority to obey. PCRC security forces were deployed around the state to control the outbreak. Containment teams rounded up the infected for transport to quarantine zones. All universities in the state were closed and taken over by the state via eminent domain to be turned into holding areas to house the infected until a cure could be found. For the rest of the population, personal restrictions in movement and activities were enforced as part of the statewide enactment of martial law.

Sure, there were a few hiccups. After the nation viewed the President of the United States and the Congress and Senate devouring each other on live TV, the public became understandably concerned. The White House in Washington, D.C. was overrun with panicked and angry citizens, and while the Secret Service was eventually able to secure the building, it sustained severe damage. Perfunctory looting and mass civil unrest occurred in parts of the nation, but the National Guard and local first responders took control, and calm and civility was again restored. For most of the nation, life went on as normal, except for a couple troubled spots: Texas, California, and, of course, New Jersey.

PCRC was granted the sole source contract to provide security and restoration of operations for the state of NJ, which bore the brunt of much of the mayhem. Due to the unprecedented nature of events, unprecedented actions were needed and regulations were created and strictly enforced.

While the rest of the country was handled by local elected officials and law enforcement, New Jersey, which was now the temporary seat of power in the country, was completely under the control of the PCRC.

The last of the official US military presence within NJ was a temporarily established Forward Operating Base, or FOB, at Princeton University. This outpost was given the name FOB Prince, but the soldiers stationed there called it FOB Brains. It was to serve as the beachhead for the initial military response to the Skell outbreak. In command of this base was Colonel James Tindall. Events overcame the colonel and the end result was the calling in of an illegal air strike against chemical plants in Northern New Jersey. The Colonel had believed all was lost, and that the resulting toxic chemical plume from the strike would wipe out the Skells, as well as much of the uninfected, across NJ. But he did not plot the winds before launch and much of the chemical cloud drifted away from the state. Sorry, New York. After that, Col. Tindall fled and became a wanted man.

California was also in chaos, but not for any Skell-related reasons. For over a year, a domestic terror group had taken root in Northern California. They called themselves G.R.A.SS, which stood for Green

Rights Action, Schutzstaffel. Their followers were a loosely knit amalgam of outsiders with opposing, and even contradictory, gripes and demands who found commonality under the GRASS banner. There were anti-capitalists, anti-government, and general anarchists. Skinheads, and hippies, hackers and anti-technologists, anti-immigration groups and Hispanic gangs, and all religions from Atheists to Zoroastrians. Together, they had traveled from across the nation, and even from across the globe, to join the GRASS terrorist movement. By sheer numbers alone, they had turned much of Northern California into a law enforcement no-go zone. These new followers, some street thugs, some technical cyber guru's, some media savvy propagandists, took to calling themselves The Blades of GRASS.

There were sporadic reports of outbreaks and attacks outside of New Jersey. Some were unsubstantiated rumors, some were premeditated murders arranged to look like Skell attacks, and some were confirmed Skell infections, most likely caused by infected who had managed to leave New Jersey before it was sealed off from the rest of the world. Some sick-minded individuals empathized with the Skells, and while not infected themselves, saw the infected as a type of grassroots uprising. Some even went out and committed their own atrocities, which were referred to in the media as "Skell Inspired Attacks."

Only a few people knew the true series of events that unleashed the Skell apocalypse, for the rest it was still a mystery.

As for the boys of Holy Family School, they were scattered, battered, and confused.

Congressman Patrick Callahan, now the sole-surviving elected official of the federal government, was sworn into the presidency at the Congress Hotel located in Cape May, NJ, thus ensuring the continuity of government.

The new president's first action was to declare the entire state of New Jersey a disaster area and establish martial law.

The Skell virus itself was released when lab-grown meat, created from human stem cells, was unintentionally distributed throughout New Jersey. Once the genie was out of the bottle, a shadowy organization pumped the rest of the meat supply out where it could be consumed.

Few knew that the stem cells used to create the Modified Embolic Animal Tissue came from the now-President Patrick Callahan. Once the infected heard his voice, it was as if they sensed that he was the source, their progenitor, and they entered a trance-like state.

PCRC used this method to calm the infected and neutralized the zombie hordes in populated areas with deployed Kraken systems. These audio units were large shipping containers, each the size of a freight train car, and referred to as "Kraken" because of their telescoping pole with loudspeakers that rose from the top of the unit. The boxes also contained computer-controlled miniguns, which would pop out and mow down rampaging Skells or humans that were either attempting to flee the state or tamper with the boxes. They were parachuted in during the original outbreak, and more were delivered via PCRC transport trucks and placed in strategic locations.

Every main artery leading out of the state had received at least two or three of them. Every bridge, tunnel, and highway had containers placed. All the airports as well. Anyone who was in New Jersey prior to the outbreak, was, for now, a prisoner in New Jersey.

Once the Kraken was activated, it emitted a hum. That hum became so pervasive that it was soon unnoticed by the general public. But, to the infected, the sound mimicked the tone and vocal inflection of President Callahan's voice. In the immediate area surrounding those boxes, the Skells assembled, drawn to the calming sound, which ceased their crazed flesh eating attacks. They congregated, mesmerized and mollified by the sound, thus allowing the PCRC Containment Teams to round them up into large white trucks for transport to FEMA quarantine camps, where they would be housed until a cure could be found.

FEMA had established several such camps by taking over the state's universities and colleges. These camps were heavily guarded by PCRC Security Forces to ensure that the infected did not escape and to protect the infected from angry, frightened citizens who wished to harm or kill these poor unfortunates.

At least that was what the public was told.

The initial camps were set up at Princeton University and The College of New Jersey, as their on-site dorm facilities would be used as makeshift hospital wards. Also on campus, large white single story "triage" buildings were erected on the main campus quads for intake and examination of new arrivals.

Announcements went out via TV, radio, and all social media of the importance of notifying the authorities of your family member, neighbor, friend or coworker showed signs of infection. The message warned that the quarantine camps were their only hope of cure and if Skells remained out in the open, they faced state-sanctioned elimination or vigilante killings.

A large trucking center called TransWays, which was off the southern portion of the NJ Turnpike, was also taken over by the state for logistics planning. This massive single story building had dozens of bay doors lining each side of the facility, allowing up to one hundred trucks at a time to back up and unload their dangerous cargo.

As for much of the rural areas of the state, it was still chaotic. The Skells were still running rampant and spreading the virus. Containment Teams and Kraken audio stations were only being deployed to more populous regions and cities. In the non-populous areas, people were on their own, told to stay indoors until their properties could be cleared of Skells by Containment Teams. They were instructed to listen to daily radio updates by Dr. Zed, who provided survival tips and mass Skell movement updates. These announcements were not much different from weather updates prior to a large incoming snowstorm. Information would be shared on where large herds of Skells were located, what direction they were moving towards, and approximate times they would be passing through towns so that residents had enough warning to run their errands and stock up on food and medicine before the Skell storm hit—sometimes, people could be trapped inside for a couple days when the horde was particularly large.

With the Skells seemingly under control, and PCRC clean up underway, a few hearty citizens even ventured out to walk among the infected, realizing that as long as the creatures were in earshot of the loudspeakers emitting the continuous low hum, they were docile.

President Callahan was located in his temporary New Jersey version of the White House. The government had taken over the Congress Hotel in Cape May. Serving alongside Patrick was Maxwell Gold. There were whispers in the hallways that while Patrick occupied the presidency, he was merely a proxy for Maxwell, who was really running the show. Maxwell Gold did not need to be President of the United States, he was president of PCRC, which currently was a more powerful position than the Commander in Chief, at least within the state of New Jersey. While Maxwell had plans to take his NJ security model and deploy it to the rest of the country, for now, he continued to fulfill the same role for Patrick that he had for all of the Holy Family boys over the past several decades: serving as fatherly confidant, advisor, and guardian.

Patrick was safely entombed within the de-facto garden state White House, solving the problems of a shaken country. He thought of his childhood friends and what they had been through the past week. He had asked for his intelligence team for a report on their locations.

He knew Daniel Sullivan and Black Malcolm White (BMW) had landed their helicopter and were most likely still nearby. With travel outside of the state impossible, he assumed they were still in the area. He knew Jerry Sullivan was dead, having been killed by agents from some unknown organization. He had heard reports that both Police Detective Sean McGreevy and NJ Mob Boss Virgil "Big V" Ganado were unaccounted for and presumed dead.

He was aware that Dr. Woodrow Coleman had escaped the PCRC lab prior to its destruction and had shown up at Forward Operating Base Prince, along with a lab scientist named Mohammed Ghazi and night security guard Jack "Smoothie" Jones.

A PCRC Security Team was dispatched to take over FOB Prince and arrest Colonel Tindall, but found only a few of his men left behind. He had escaped and was followed by a group of soldiers loyal to him.

Ivan Gold and his wife Marifi had fled their hideout at the former Chadwick Manor. PCRC Security had been dispatched to the site once they learned about it from Patrick Callahan, but when they arrived, they only found a burned out mansion, the remains of Gerald Sullivan, and many other dead and infected around the campus.

3
TWO ZOMBIES WALK INTO A BAR

Daniel Sullivan and Malcom White, AKA Black Malcom White, AKA, BMW, had hunkered down at The Shore Thing Bar and Grill, just off Cape May's Beachside Drive. They were joined by about a dozen other souls who were either brave enough or desperate enough for a cocktail to leave their homes and seek refuge in the low-end bar. Most drank their beers and liquor in silence while staring at the TV monitors suspended from the ceilings above the circular bar. Vacant eyes and slack jaws, staring at the monitors above the bar like it was the last thirty seconds of a tied-score Super Bowl, or the final rose ceremony of The Bachelor, whichever your preference. As Daniel glanced around the bar at the shell-shocked drunks, they did not appear much different from the very zombies they were watching being rounded up on TV.

News anchors from around the country discussed the Jersey pandemic, the incident in Washington, DC, the presidential transition of power to a young, novice congressman, and when, or if, New Jersey borders would ever be reopened. There was a growing sentiment in the rest of the country that NJ should stay sealed off for good—maybe even wiped off the planet.

Field journalists were "coming to you live" from the land of the dammed. They reported from military blockades just north of Jersey, displaying heavy weaponry that the National Guard had brought in to ensure no one entered or exited the state alive. Behind those reporters, rowdy crowds chanted and held up signs. Catchy, empty slogans always seemed to follow a national tragedy, such as Give Peace a Chance, Support Our Troops or COEXIST. The only bumper sticker slogan that fit this mess was Shit Happens.

The front door of The Shore Thing bar swung open, startling the jittery customers. One patron fell backwards off his bar stool. The bartender grabbed his shotgun and pointed it at the door, ready to blow away any incoming Skell. The burst of sunshine that exploded behind the visitor made it difficult to tell friend from foe for a few seconds until everyone's eyes adjusted.

"*Whoaaah* there, barkeep," said the new guest, "lower your weapon." A tall, clean cut paramilitary man entered with a confident swagger. Behind him was another man, dressed in the same fatigues, shorter in stature, but with the kind of muscular build that comes from a vial and needle in the ass cheek. This man had his gun drawn in front of him and was ready, if not eager, to shoot anyone he perceived a threat. He looked one sideways glance away from roid rage.

As the door closed and eyes adjusted, the two visitors became fully visible. By their uniforms, they were PCRC private contractors. The tall one walked over to Daniel. "Mr. Sullivan, would you please accompany me outside, we need to talk." He said in a polite, professional, and calm tone.

"I am perfectly comfortable here at the bar. Why don't you say what you have to say? We can talk over a beer," Daniel offered. He looked over at the second man. "I'll order a Cosmo for your date," he said with a nod to the gunslinger.

"Fuck you, Sullivan!" was the response from Mr. Cosmo.

Daniel recognized the voice. It was Bankowski. He and Malcolm had played football against Bankowski in high school. The guy was a miserable prick back then and apparently had not changed. Neither of the two men had any identifying name or rank on their uniforms, just numbers. Tall, calm guy was 7322. The douchebag was 0303.

Not enough zeros for that loser's name, Daniel thought.

"Mr. Sullivan, if you would step outside with us. Please." The tall man requested again with exceeding politeness and not a sense of threat or attempted intimidation.

Daniel was unsure why, but this guy did not want to have an issue in the bar, at least not one with witnesses. His demeanor did put Daniel at ease, even though the man's partner seemed itching for a fight.

Daniel and BMW stood up and walked out the door, followed by the two PCRC contractors. They were met in the parking lot by eight more contractors. These were PCRC security teams, not containment teams. They were all heavily armed and standing next to two HUMVEEs. Just beyond them, about two dozen Skells had gathered around a shipping container that was still propped up on a trailer hitch. The contractors had towed it with them and then unhitched it in an adjacent parking lot. More zombies were staggering towards the device, drawn to its sound, unaware or uninterested in the human buffet that was mere feet away.

Daniel recalled seeing dozens of similar containers parachuted in during the initial outbreak. They had been dropped from low altitude aircraft and drifted down like giant steel encased, heavily weaponized, two-ton snowflakes.

"Mr. Sullivan, we have been asked to escort you to a meeting with President Callahan," 7322 informed them.

Daniel smirked. *President Callahan. That is going to take some getting used to,* he thought. "Please tell Patrick to come join us at the bar. I saved his ass from getting kicked too many times to be summoned," Daniel responded. "Also, tell Patrick he's buying. Oh, excuse me, tell *Mr. President* he's buying."

BMW leaned towards Daniel. "We should go. May be the best way to find out what the hell is going on."

"What do you mean *we?*" 0303 snapped at BMW. "No one has been addressing you, *White,*" 0303 said with emphasis on Malcolm's surname

Malcolm White took a step towards 0303, which caused 0303 to again raise his gun. Malcolm quickly drew his own .45 and Daniel pulled out his Glock.

All remained frozen.

"Well, well, looks like we have a Mexican standoff," 0303 said.

"Better watch those words, there Bankowski, that term could be considered racially insensitive," BMW chastised.

7322 shouted: "Can we cut the school yard bullshit and put the guns away?" He looked over at 0303. "All of you!"

0303 reluctantly complied and lowered his weapon, as did Daniel and BMW.

With firearms holstered and calm restored, 7322 continued. "We're here to pick up Sullivan, not you, Mr. White. But if it will move things along, I am sure it is not a problem for you to come as well."

"And what if we don't?" Daniel questioned, still testing the waters.

7322 reached into his vest pocket and removed a remote control device. He pointed it at the shipping container. About eighty ragged, skeletal creatures had now surrounded it. He pushed a button on the small remote, which caused the hum from the device to cease. It was only when the hum vanished that Daniel and BMW realized it has been there at all. The sound had just become so common you did not notice or think about it, until it was no more. Like a woman you only realize you love when she leaves you.

It took mere seconds for the Skells surrounding the device to also realize the hum that attracted them was gone and to snap out of their trance. They began looking around, confused, sniffing the air. One by one, they noticed the men standing outside the bar. Their heads tilted and long lines of drool seeped out of their gaping maws. Their dead eyes widened with desire as they all began moving steadily towards the assembled crew outside The Shore Thing bar entrance. The other PCRC security contractors calmly stepped back inside their armored Humvees and shut the doors, safe inside from the descending group of flesh eaters. Daniel looked over his shoulder and saw the terrified faces of the bar patrons pressed up against the windows, watching what was unfolding. They could see the staggering horde of unwanted guests heading towards the establishment.

"You can probably fight them off, and maybe one or both of you will get away," 7322 said. "But your friends in the bar there will be dinner. Your decision."

"Okay, okay, shit, I'll go," Daniel responded.

7322 clicked the remote again and the hum resumed. The creatures immediately turned and stared at the contraption. Obviously, there was no rush to round up or exterminate all of the infected if they were being used to keep the civilians compliant and fearful.

Daniel said, "One condition. After I meet with him, we need fuel for BMW's chopper."

"Man, look what we have here," 0303 said loudly so the contractors in the vehicles could hear. "A cowardly Irishman and a flying monkey. We must be in the Land of Oz."

Daniel and BMW did not need to exchange looks. Both knew what they both were going to do next.

That was the final straw.

In a flash, they were both on top of 0303, kicking his ass. BMW leveled him with a right cross and before the idiot realized what was happening, BMW was on top of him, raining down blows. Meanwhile, Daniel was scoring field goals with the prone man's balls, kicking him between his flailing legs.

The other contractors stepped out of their vehicles, but didn't approach, as nobody wanted to be on the receiving end of this beat down.

It was a trick that the Sullivan boys had perfected in high school and had taught the rest of their motley crew of friends. Whenever threatened by a group that outnumbered them, they would not try to take on their foes one by one. That was sure to lead to defeat. Instead, all of the boys—Daniel, Gerald, Patrick, Ivan, Sean, Stephen, Virgil, Malcolm—would together jump the biggest guy, or whomever was the main instigator, and pummel him. Leave all the others alone, just dogpile on that one guy who was shooting off his mouth. Nine times out of ten, the rest of the opposing group would either flee or stand there and not jump in. It was typical that a majority of an opposing gang did not really want to fight, that it was just one or two assholes who were pushing them along.

This was one of those times. These other men were not soldiers who saw a comrade down. They were paid mercenaries, working for Maxwell Gold, and if they were not told to take an action or make a decision, they wouldn't. They did not give a shit about 0303—there was no brotherhood here, just rent-a-cops.

"All right, knock it off, you assholes!" 7322 shouted as he reached down and pulled BMW off his humbled cohort, while giving Daniel a push backwards. "0303, get in the goddamn vehicle!" He shouted. "You two," he said, pointing at a chuckling Daniel and BMW. "You two ride with me. Like dealing with fucking children here!"

"He started it," Dan said sheepishly as he and BMW climbed into the back of 7322's Humvee.

4
NETWORK IS DOWN

Wizard-Ware was a white hat hacking firm. As far as cybercrime went, "white hats" would advise the US government on the ways of criminal hackers while "black hats" would exploit secure systems.

Ronan, Majesty and Lars entered the small Los Angeles office of Wizard-Ware. They stopped in the middle of the small reception area where a young female receptionist waited at a glass desk. She flipped through her iPhone and, without looking up, instructed them to sign in using an iPad nearby.

She never saw the gun that put the bullet through her head.

Two men ran out from a door behind the now deceased millennial and they too were shot dead.

Ronan, Majesty, and Lars stepped over the dead men's bodies and walked through. A half dozen more twenty-somethings cowered behind computer workstations.

"Mr. Barnes," Ronan called out. "I am seeking the elusive Mr. Barnes."

There was silence in the room other than the weak sound from the headphones of a Zune that had fallen to the ground.

Majesty looked at the rare device. "A Zune? Really?" she said to the cowering man with the neck beard who obviously had dropped it. "What, are you trying to be unique or something? Some sort of way to stand out?" She shot him in his beard.

Lars walked over and pointed the gun at the heavyset nerd next to him. "You. Recite a verse from the Koran."

"W-w-w...what?" the terrified and confused man asked.

"Recite a verse from the Koran and I will let you live," Lars repeated.

"I...I don't know any verses. I'm not a Muslim," the man whimpered.

"Dude. I'm just fucking with you." Lars laughed. "Do we look like camel jockeys to you?" Lars shot the man in the head.

"How many more have to die before I meet the elusive Mr. Barnes?" Ronan yelled out.

A slender man in his thirties rose up with his hands raised. "I am George Barnes," he said, voice quivering.

"Ahh, Mr. Barnes." Ronan sneered. "How long I have been trying to reach you. I call, I email you, I leave you messages on the dark web, yet you don't respond."

"I don't know who you are." Barnes replied.

"Who I am does not matter. Who *we* are is what matters. We are GRASS. And you have been trying to thwart us. Isn't that true?"

Barnes did not respond. His eyelids became slits.

Ronan sniffed. "Working for the man, every night and day. All your talent. What a waste."

Barnes and Wizard-Ware had been hired by the NSA to track and cyber infiltrate GRASS prior to the Skell virus.

"Well, I get it," Ronan continued. "We are all trying to make a buck in this capitalist system. It's not that you worked for the government. That didn't bother me. It's not that you tried to infiltrate my organization and hack into my networks that bothered me." He smiled. "Actually, I was flattered by the attention. What bothered me was that you would not respond to me, elusive Mr. Barnes. Soon, everyone will respond to me. Kings, presidents, dictators will take my call. But you, the elusive Mr. Barnes, put me on the 'Pay No Mind list.' It hurt."

Barnes did not know what to say. "I'm... I'm sorry?" he said meekly. Confused.

Ronan's grin spread from ear to ear. "Apology accepted!" he declared. "Now we can become friends. And as friends, I want you to share something with me. Something that will spare the life of these remaining employees. Nothing much. Just a little bit of code. A few ones and zeros. That is all I need. A little bit of code for a little program that I know you helped develop. That sounds like a fair swap for the lives of your people, doesn't it?

Barnes nodded.

"Good. Now, my associate here will be securing your people in the server room while you and I have a little SCRUM meeting."

Lars waved his gun and hustled the remaining staff through a door in the rear. He gave Ronan the Nazi straight arm, raised hand salute, which drew a nasty glare from Majesty.

"Ugh," she groaned and gave Lars the finger.

Ronan turned to his beloved. "Majesty, please take Mr. Barnes down to our car and be sure he brings his laptop. Oh, and don't forget your power cord. I hate when I leave for a trip and I forget my laptop's power cord."

She nodded in agreement and ushered the man out of the front door.

As Lars was locking the server door with the remaining staff inside, Ronan approached him angrily.

"Dude, will you knock off that Hitler shit. At least in front of my girlfriend?" He snapped.

Lars, a muscular man in his early twenties with a shaved head, stood his ground. "Hey man, this is what we're about. I don't feel comfortable with the Jewish presence."

Ronan stood his ground too. "First off, *Laurence*," Ronan said with an emphasis on his counterpart's real name, not the more Germanic-sounding moniker he had started calling himself, "I am in charge here. You chose to follow me. And we are a secular collective. So knock off the Jew and Nazi shit. Don't forget, your parents were Scientologists. If I didn't come into your life, you would be worshiping Tom Cruise."

Lars/Laurence was angry, but chastened. "Yeah, yeah. Okay. Let's go before the cops get here." He changed the subject. "You think this guy has the code we need?"

"I'm sure of it. I just need to figure out once I get it, how I deploy it. But don't worry—something or someone will show us the way. After all, we are GRASS." Ronan put his hand on the back of Lars's neck to show there were no hard feelings.

5
HIDING THE WOODY

Dr. Woodrow peered through the child's telescope he found in the abandoned second story bedroom. He, Mohammed, and their tag along night watchman Smoothie had followed Colonel Tindall and his men after they evacuated FOB Prince. They had taken up residence in several well-appointed, yet recently abandoned, houses at the end of a cul-de-sac. The neighborhood was posh, with houses possibly running in the millions of dollars. All of which had been evacuated by their former owners when PCRC contractors came and cordoned off the area surrounding Princeton campus. The once-prestigious university, which became a temporary military base, had now become a quarantine camp. White box trucks with the PCRC Containment Force logo rolled in carrying their dangerous cargo of infected, and rolled out empty to pick up fresh meat. Also rolling in were cylindrical tanker trucks. Lots of them. *Perhaps fuel,* Woodrow thought. But by the sheer quantity of trucks, he could not imagine what their cargo could be.

In the center of campus, he could see a large, single story structure. It had no windows that he could see.

There were black uniformed soldiers clearing out the remaining infected from areas surrounding the campus. Those that were found were restrained and shoved into the PCRC box trucks. Other security teams were moving from building to building. They were searching, and Woodrow knew who for. They were looking for Colonel Tindall. The houses that had already been searched had markings on the side to indicate they were empty. So it would be some time before crews came back for a second look. At least, Woodrow hoped so.

Woodrow, Mohammed, and Smoothie had found refuge at FOB Prince after escaping the PCRC building and being picked up on the side of the road by Reverend Bob. Things went south when Colonel Tindall asked the reverend to pray alongside his wife, who had become infected and turned Skell. The colonel walked in to find Rev. Bob administering more than last rights to his wife. Tindall's mind snapped, and in a fit of madness, he killed the reverend and put his wife out of her misery. He then proactively called in the ill-timed strike on the chemical plants.

A once-respected military officer, Tindall was now a fugitive. About three dozen of his soldiers remained loyal to him, and rather than becoming conscripted into the PCRC security forces which now controlled the state. They followed Colonel Tindall and had hunkered down in abandoned houses waiting for his next move. He had instilled something within them. Although they did not know what they were going to do, they knew they should be following this man.

Woodrow believed it was better that he, too, kept in the safety of Colonel Tindall's soldiers. Unlike the rent-a-thug contractors that were tearing apart buildings and hauling off Skells around the neighborhoods, these men were professional soldiers, heavily armed, and they had an innate sense to protect those that could not defend themselves.

Woodrow had manipulated such men for his own protection since he could remember. Growing up, he had a weak body, but a strong mind, a quick wit, and a sharp tongue. He loved to poke the power structure in the eye. In high school, he would mock the jocks and face-men. Provoking these bullies through insults and exposing their dimness to shrieks of laughter from the girls. Once the objects of his insults could take no more and moved in to pound him, he would run and hide behind the Sullivan brothers, who were always eager for a fight. It was a great symbiotic relationship. He provided them laughs and they provided him protection. But they were gone now, the enemy was much more dangerous, and the consequences would be more than broken eye glasses and a black eye. He needed someone to protect him, to fight his battles, and right now, Tindall's men would do nicely.

6

911

Operator: Hello, 911, what is your emergency.

Caller: Yeah, I got like three of those fucking zombies on my lawn.

Operator: Sir, they are infected, not zombies. Please provide me your address.

Caller: Or Skells, isn't that what they're calling these skinny fucks?

Operator: Sir, you do not need to use foul language. Is your house secured, are you or anyone else in immediate danger?

Caller: I'm in my living room, these things are on my lawn. They're the ones in immediate danger. I can go out and bash their fucking heads in right now, leave a nice pile for you to come clean up.

Operator: Sir, please do not leave your house or engage with the infected. I have pulled up your address from our system based on your phone number and we will be sending a containment team out to your location right now.

Caller: Save your gas, honey, I've been watching these dumb fucks and they don't seem to wily. I think I can clean them out myself. Leave them on the curb for Monday's pick up.

Operator: Sir, again, I am telling you not to leave your house or to interact with the infected in any way.

Caller: Um, do you think they'd be picked up during trash day or during recycling day? So ridiculous having to put out bottles and cans on their own day. My garage stinks from soup cans and beer bottle residue. Fucking tree huggers.

Operator: Sir, I have asked you to refrain from foul language, and also, you will be committing a felony if you purposely go out and harm or kill the infected.

Caller: They're dead already, I can just go out and put them down.

Operator: Sir, I said—

Caller: Hold on, honey, I'll be right back.

Operator: Sir, I am telling you containment will be there in less than a minute.

Caller: Gotta go kill these zombies.

Operator: Sir? Sir! ...Sir?

Unknown voice: Hello?

Operator: Sir, I am asking you not to leave your—

Unknown voice: Hold on, ma'am, this is PCRC Officer 0401, who am I speaking with?

Operator: Thank goodness. This is the 911 operator, please tell the caller not to leave his house.

PCRC Officer 0401: Oh, you're probably referring to the homeowner. He's dead. We are cleaning up the situation now. Is that all?

Operator: Yes. Yes, I have other calls to take. Fucking rednecks.

7
MAN'S BEST FRIEND

The Cape May-based Congress Hotel, now home to the temporary Oval Office, was like a fortress. The streets surrounding the building were sealed off and those living there had been relocated. Outside, a safe-zone had been established. The perimeter was comprised of wooden barricades, triple concertina wire fencing, and guard dogs. Just outside the concentric circles of barricades were frightened and angry citizens. They chanted, yelled, and prayed. Some with signs demanding answers or large placards accusing the new president of orchestrating the crisis himself to usurp power. Some hauled large crucifixes and pleaded with people to repent, that the end of days was upon us. All religions were represented in different segments of the crowd. Bowing, kneeling, wailing, singing or just standing still in silent prayer. A complete diversity of divine fervor.

Meanwhile, others went about their normal life as if nothing had happened. Stores, restaurants, and bars were open for business.

Inside the hotel, things were equally frenetic, with furniture being moved, phones ringing, military leaders convening, senior government officials and low level aides rushing through the halls. BMW was escorted by one of the PCRC security team to the hotel bar, which was now also serving as the press area. Dan was escorted by 7322 to the transitory Oval Office.

Men and women, paramilitary types, clad in black tactical uniforms, lined the hallways. Secret service or uniformed police were nowhere to be seen.

Patrick was seated behind the desk of what was once a luxury suite of the hotel as Daniel was escorted in. Lining the wall of the office were a half dozen more armor-clad PCRC security members, protecting, and perhaps monitoring, the new president.

It had only been two weeks, yet Patrick looked as if he had aged a decade. He was thin and somewhat withered. It seemed as if a strong wind could carry him away. He was a Flat Stanley version of Commander in Chief.

A man in a brown suit stood in front of Patrick's desk holding a binder tightly in his clasped hands. He had been providing a briefing for the president, but immediately stopped and closed the binder when Dan walked into the room.

Patrick raised his hand as if to ease the concern of the brown suit-wearing man. He then smiled weakly at Daniel and gestured for his old friend to sit in the leather chair in front of the desk. Daniel complied and sat down while 7322 went on to stand at parade rest near the back of the room.

Patrick returned his attention to the briefing. "That's okay, Mr. Spencer, please continue what you were saying. I requested Mr. Sullivan come here. It is important that he understand what is going on and the magnitude of what we are dealing with here."

As Spencer started to reopen the folder to resume the briefing, he hesitated, giving a sideways look at the slightly disheveled Daniel Sullivan.

"Mr. Spencer, you may speak freely," Patrick assured. "He is a friend."

Spencer replied sarcastically, "Sir, you're the president now. It's an isolating position. If you really want a friend, I suggest you get a dog."

Patrick smiled. "I already have one." He gave head nod and a knowing wink in the direction of Daniel.

"I feel like a mutt moving from one master to another," Daniel muttered to himself.

Spencer continued his briefing. "We have a formal state of emergency declared for the entirety of New Jersey. We currently have control of all ingress and egress points of the state. We have had to severely restrict the movement of persons within our borders, temporarily, with curfew from six p.m. until eight a.m. During non-curfew hours, the populace has been requested to stay off the streets in areas not yet cleared by our containment teams. This executive order is due to the occurring phenomena, and the public has been told these rules are to prevent, or at least minimize, loss of life."

Patrick said, "I want to ensure we are following the rule of law and not overstepping our bounds. Are we following all existing procedures for these executive actions?" He sounded like a Boy Scout.

"Sir, yes," Spencer continued. "You have the right to declare a state of emergency in the event of, but not exclusive to, infestations, riots, sabotage, hostile military or paramilitary action, bioterrorism, or incidents involving weapons of mass destruction. We have most of those occurring all at once right now. No one of reason would express concern over the actions we have taken in light of these most...unusual circumstances."

"I understand," Patrick said. "I just want to be clear that this is being handled no differently than we would handle a pandemic, an earthquake, a flood or any other large scale response. Please continue Mr. Spencer."

Spencer nodded. "Currently, we have eleven counties in New Jersey with confirmed infection." He looked over his briefing notes. "We have fifteen counties quarantined, including the prior mentioned eleven, the other four as a precaution due to *un*confirmed reports of outbreak.

"We have seven additional counties under surveillance for unconfirmed sightings. Lots of false reports, hoaxes, and people abusing the circumstance to make false reports or cause trouble or settle scores."

Spencer flapped a hand. "People reporting their ex-spouses and bosses. That kind of thing. No crisis goes to waste for some people."

"Dr. Reynolds." Patrick said to some unknown person.

A female voice sounded off: "The infected are much more resilient than you or I, and despite their frail, skeletal appearance, they are quite strong, fast, and when not in stasis mode, difficult to restrain."

Daniel did not realize where the voice was coming from at first, but then saw a small, prim looking woman sitting just to the right or Spencer. She was so slight and easy to miss that it barely seemed like she was in the room.

Dr. Reynolds spoke clinically. "It is important that we keep informing the people that this is *not* some sort of supernatural event or biblical prophecy or the dead coming back to life. There is also no such indication that this is some sort of outside terrorist attack. This is a virus, a particularly virulent and unusual one, which causes those infected to commit horrific atrocities, but in the end, it is just a virus."

Her voice remained as flat and scientific tonally as someone whose world consisted of books and beakers. "We are securing the infected so that they can be transported and housed in quarantine until we can cure them, or reverse the process that has taken over their bodies. We are working within FEMA guidelines to establish these camps around the state, which will ensure the safety of both the infected and the uninfected population."

"Dr. Reynolds, how close are we to a cure?" Patrick inquired.

"Unfortunately, much of the team and their research was lost when the original PCRC test facility was destroyed. We need to find Dr. Coleman to assist in the reverse engineering of this virus."

Mr. Spencer spoke up. "We are still looking for Colonel Tindall as well. We are unclear as to why he prematurely called in the missile attack, although it would appear from what we found at the base that some disturbing event had occurred. We hope he's not compromised and we have been putting out messages that he is not the target of prosecution, we just need to know what happened. Once we have him, though, he will have to face trial for what he has done."

Patrick sighed. "So you put out word that if he turns himself in, we won't prosecute, yet if he does, we will prosecute him as a war criminal. So basically, we're lying, correct?"

"I guess Ivan was right," Daniel chimed in. "You really can't trust the government."

Patrick shot Daniel a quick look with a clear message: *Shut the fuck up.* "Mr. Spencer, any additional good news to share?"

Mr. Spencer flipped the pages in his binder. He took a deep breath. "Texas announced that they officially seceded from the United States and become the independent Republic of Texas. More troubling is that they have had some skirmishes at the border with the Mexicans. We are consulting with the State Department and Pentagon to consider our options and what can be done before this turns into a shooting war."

Patrick stood up and looked out the window of his new office. "Okay, so we have gassed New York, lost Texas, potentially started a war with Mexico, and flooded New Jersey with zombies. What about the rest of the country?"

Spencer turned another page. "Well, sir, California has become very problematic, but the rest of this briefing is classified top secret. I need to meet with Mr. Gold right now, but I will resume our briefing after you complete your meeting with your friend and we can discuss the West Coast situation."

Patrick relented. He needed a break from the barrage of bad news. "Thank you, Mr. Spencer. Oh, by the way, any update on locating the governor? I heard a rumor he had been found."

Mr. Spencer smirked. "That report was a false alarm. A man entered a police station yesterday in Trenton claiming to be the governor. He had his spiel down pat, seemed to know a lot that only the governor would know. There was even a slight resemblance. The issue was this imposter was only about a hundred and ten pounds soaking wet. While he looked like the governor, and had all his facts accurate, you'd think the guy would have tried to add some padding to pull off the look. But, honestly, sir, we have thousands of missing person reports, we have portions of the state that are totally overrun, they are considered no-go zones. If he is out there, we will find him."

Mr. Spencer left the room to head to his briefing of Maxwell Gold.

"Dr. Reynolds, do you have anything to add?" Patrick asked, curious as to why the woman was still sitting there.

She did not respond. She was lost in thought, as if she were trying to figure a way to say something. Or tell someone something they did not want to say out loud. Daniel recognized that look. It was the look you got telling a girl you'd screwed that she might want to get herself to the gynecologist for an STD test.

"Dr. Reynolds?" Patrick repeated.

The doctor breathed in and opened her mouth. Daniel realized at that moment how attractive she was. And not just in an "I've been fighting zombies and the only naked woman I have seen in a week was an infected woman running down the street resembling a skeleton wearing a latex bodysuit made out of skin" attractive, but teen movie, take off the dork glasses, pull the hair out of the tight bun, and *voila*: attractive.

"Reynolds!" the shout came from Mr. Spencer, who had returned and was poking his head back through the door.

Dr. Reynolds got up and scurried out of the room, followed by Spencer, who shut the door behind them.

"They make a cute couple," Daniel said.

8
SWIPE RIGHT

This is Dr. Zed coming to you with your Outbreak Update.

Even in the face of the zombie apocalypse, tech entrepreneurs still keep innovating. A brand new app has been developed by the Post Conflict Restoration Corp and is being pushed out to *all* smart phones as a software update. There will be no charge for this app and your data plan will not be billed.

The app is called WALKR and you'll see the icon once your phone restarts. To use the app, just click WALKR on your smart phone, then take a picture of an infected or suspected infected. Once you have a photo, swipe the photo to the right, and it'll be sent to the PCRC Containment Team headquarters. The photo will be automatically tagged with the latitude and longitude of where it was taken, allowing PCRC Containment Teams to arrive within minutes to collect the infected for safe transport to a quarantine camp. There, the infected will be well cared for until a cure can be found and administered. If you did not get a good photo, or you realize the picture is *not* a Skell but really your ex-wife or mother-in-law, simply swipe left, and the photo will be deleted.

And please folks, stop sending in pictures of Gwyneth Paltrow, she is not a Skell, she's a vegan! Just a little joke there, Gwyn, no need to call the lawyers!

Now, Dr. Zed says: please don't confuse this with that other swiping app, otherwise you could end up dating a *real stiff.*

Unlike that other app, WALKR is meant to *stop* the spread of disease.

Dr. Zed is just joking folks—infection control is everyone's responsibility.

We now return to your regular programming.

9
LOST

Fiona gazed out the window of the passenger side of her brother James Sullivan's car. He had picked her up from the small airport where a private PCRC jet had flown her in from her home in Washington, DC. She had left—some may say fled—Jersey for D.C. only a couple years prior, but you never really leave New Jersey. It can't be scrubbed off you, it can't be purged out of you; it is in your DNA.

Since leaving, she had returned at most twice a year, and when she did, it would appear as if she never left. Same crowd at the T-Bone Bar, same high school, same roads, same shops. Yet this time, it was as if she were in a version of her hometown only seen in nightmares. A landscape recognizable, yet unfamiliar. She was lost.

She had been brought back to her hometown by Maxwell in an attempt to provide some comfort for her brother James. She hoped that, while there, she would gain some closure for herself as well.

She and James were two damaged people, bonded by blood, but distant as strangers. She had grown closer to her brother Gerald when he shared his secret with her not long ago. It was a vulnerability he exposed which had brought her closer to him than either of her other two brothers. The death of Gerald had crushed her emotionally, but it seemed to cause James to snap. He was not a man unaccustomed to death. While her brother Daniel was relentless in his recounting of war stories, relishing in every act of valor or depravity, James had not spoken much about his time in special operations or of his work as a mercenary for PCRC.

Growing up, she observed her older brothers as if she was researching primates in the wild. She saw how their core group of friends had formed, and she alone had sensed the invisible hand of Maxwell Gold coaxing them together, and then serving as a shepherd, guiding each of them into their individual—possibly pre-determined—destiny. It was not until recently that she had understood why he took such interest, and why he had shaped and coalesced them to suit his anticipated future needs.

Her eyes turned to a large green freeway exit sign in the distance. James Sullivan saw it as well and slowed the car to view the spectacle. Underneath the white letters that read North Exit, someone had spray painted: "Must Gut Them!"

It was not the first time she had seen that simple, three-word command scrawled.

Must gut them.

It had been written on brick walls, written in huge letters across the asphalt of a Kmart parking lot. It was not until this moment that she realized what that three-word message was commanding them to do. Beyond the sign, positioned on the side of the road, three Skells had been propped against highway equipment.

Their stomachs sliced open, their black, oily intestines laying in a pile on the ground in front of them. It was a grotesque illustration by the author to convey what he wanted done.

James realized his sister was gawking at this gruesome display and accelerated.

"I'm really glad you're here, Fi," James said, hoping to pull her attention away. "It's been a long time. I don't know what Maxwell told you, but really, I'm fine." It was a lie. "But I'm glad you're here anyway."

Fiona looked over at him. "Mr. Gold told me you tried to commit suicide."

James balked, "That's ridiculous!" He did not look over at her; he kept his eyes on the nearly empty road. Before the apocalypse, at this time of day, traffic would be at a standstill. Right now, there was barely another car on the road.

Fiona did not believe James, but she played along. "Okay, I thought it was a load of horseshit anyway." She noticed how quickly her vernacular reverted back to the way it was before she left the state. She could not speak in that fashion in gentile Washington, and it took her a while as a Jersey girl to grow accustomed to the more delicate discussions of polite society.

"So we'll be staying at the Congress hotel. Pretty swank digs. Well, for me anyway. They have the whole place locked down with a perimeter of security that a microbe couldn't penetrate. It really is the new White House."

There was activity up ahead. She saw a white truck with the PCRC logo on side. Two men in hazmat suits were using long poles with large hooks to corral half a dozen bloody Skells up a ramp into the back of the truck doors. On the side of the road, the remains of their victims. It appeared as if two cars had run off the road and the occupants were set upon by the creatures. Ripped apart and eaten. Their remains were scattered both inside and outside the vehicles.

"Do they still offer room service?" Fiona asked, figuring she would not be venturing out.

"Does the Pope shit in the woods?" James responded.

"I don't know," Fiona sighed, "but God sure shits in New Jersey."

10
COMPARTMENTALIZATION

James Sullivan had faced death many times while serving in the military and later as a mercenary. He had killed and almost been killed. He never dealt with the idea of his own mortality, though. Even in the most precarious situations, where death seemed inevitable, he knew there was at least a 1% chance he would be able to fight or shoot or talk his way out of taking a dirt nap.

Now, he was facing a foe he could not fight or shoot or talk to.

He had cancer. And to add insult to inevitability, it was MBC, male breast cancer. Inoperable, metastasized, and spreading to his heart. He had months left—optimistically.

He knew what would happen if he shared his secret. He would tell them he had breast cancer. First, they would laugh, assuming he was making a joke. Then, slowly realize was not, and their smile would fade and a look of mortification would set in. Next would come the pity, then avoidance, and from that point on, he would already be dead to them.

Why couldn't he die from something more manly, like prostate cancer, heart disease, or getting shot by a jealous husband. *Christ, male breast cancer, how fucking embarrassing,* he thought.

James had been able to file this news away, just as he had filed away the bad memories from a lifetime spent *creating* bad memories. But, as the cancer ate through his body, the thought of it ate through at the walls he had built in his mind. The "dying of cancer" compartment started to spill into the "my brother is dead" compartment.

The thoughts of cancer continued eating away his mind walls. The walls that had held back empathy, sympathy, and decency, long suppressed and hidden away, they were roaming free. They created confusion and reevaluations of decisions and past actions. Not something that someone in his line of work should ever do.

Next, the cancer thoughts began to eat through the mind walls holding long-forgotten atrocities. Atrocities he had witnessed and committed. Then it collapsed the wall that blocked out the guilty thought that he himself had paved the way for his brothers to follow in his footsteps. That he had not protected them and, instead, had led them into a life of experiencing and committing their own atrocities and war crimes.

Finally, the cancer thoughts ate through the mind wall that blocked out the faces of those he had killed and the faces of the families who cursed him. Like a horde of zombies, those thoughts and memories and faces and emotions burst through the mind walls. They descended upon him; arms out, faces ravaged, hands bloody, and teeth snapping.

His mind had made its final stand, and it had fallen.

11
THE BASE FORMERLY KNOWN AS PRINCE

Woodrow looked around the room. It appeared that the former occupant had been a teenage boy by the various swimsuit model posters and rock band promotions pinned to the walls. He saw a poster for a band called Roman Kandle, a thrash punk band based out of San Francisco.

This kid has got to have a stash of weed somewhere, he thought. *I just need to relax a bit.* He went through the kid's room, opening dresser drawers and cabinets, searching for the box or baggie that would hold the hidden buds. He found no contraband, but he did find an Apple laptop.

He opened it and the screen lit up. It automatically detected the house WiFi and went online. He needed to learn what was happening outside in the real world. He clicked over to the CNN website, then NBC, ABC, CBS, Fox. All the major news sites seemed to be reporting the same story, as if someone had handed them all the same script and they were dutiful parrots repeating what they were told to say. *For this, they are paid millions a year,* he thought.

He logged into Gmail to check his email account. He entered his username and password and his inbox opened.

There was a tone, and the Skype application opened.

"What the hell, I did not hit Skype," he muttered.

The laptop screen blurred and a video chat window overtook the display. A live feed of a man wearing a rubber cow head sitting in front of a green banner with white lettering spelling out GRASS appeared.

The rubber cow-headed person spoke to him using a voice-altering application. "Hello, Dr. Woody. We have been waiting for you."

Woodrow began to type: WHO IS THI—

"No need to type, Dr. Woody," the voice said. "You can speak freely, we can see and hear you."

Woodrow noticed that a small light next to the laptop's built in webcam was now lit. "Who are you?"

"We are the cyber arm of GRASS."

Woodrow cocked an eyebrow. "What the hell is Grass?"

"Green Rights Action, Schutzstaffel. Schutzstaffel is German for Protection Squad."

"How did you find me, how are you even doing this?"

"Again, as I just said, we are the *cyber* arm of GRASS. Is this not sinking in? We are really good at computer stuff." The cow was getting obnoxious.

"You found me when I logged into my email. Damn it!" Woodrow said it out loud, but he was cursing himself.

"You think we can't find you when you're online no matter what you're doing? We have been tracking you for months. Your phone, your car's GPS, that Fitbit on your wrist. We know where you go"

"What do you want with me?" Woodrow asked, growing more disconcerted at the tone of this conversation.

"How are you going to stop this fire, Dr. Woody?"

"You! It was you that contacted me at the lab!" Woodrow said, recalling the cryptic email he received at the PCRC underground laboratory where the Skell virus was researched and infected humans were studied.

"Yes."

"You know about the...about what was being done there," Woodrow accused.

The cow head wobbled a little. "Yes"

"Why didn't you stop it?!" Woodrow demanded.

"Why didn't *you?*"

Woodrow balled his hands into fists. "I tried!" He pleaded.

"You failed. You have a history of failing, don't you, Dr. Woody?"

"What do you want?"

"We want to help you, Dr. Woody. We want to expose the PCRC. We want to tell the world who started the zombie apocalypse."

"Okay, let's not get hyperbolic. There is no apocalypse and there are no zombies. *But,* if you want to sling mud at a corporation, do it. You don't need me. I have no affiliation with them."

"We need you to help us get the message out."

"How and why would I do that?"

"Fugitive war criminal Colonel Tindall has a laptop. That laptop has the ability to execute a specific program. Do you know if he took it with him?"

"I don't know. If not, we have no chance of getting back in there to retrieve it. The Colonel tried to gas the state. After that, we all fled. The PCRC's private army came in and stormed the base. The place is some sort of camp now. There are private contractors scurrying around everywhere like roaches."

"All we need you to do is find and turn on his laptop. On that laptop, you will find an icon that says 'Broadcast.' Double-click that icon, and together we will let the world know what is happening here in New Jersey, and what is headed their way. Everyone will know what is really happening to the infected."

Woodrow frowned. "And what is really happening?" He sensed a "we know something you don't know" shtick.

The screen on Woodrow's laptop blurred, then regained clarity to display a live video stream from cameras surrounding the Princeton University campus.

The display quickly switched from one camera to another, demonstrating that they had access to several cameras and thus, several angles.

"Do you know this place?" The voice asked.

Woodrow squinted. "Yes, that's where we were. Forward Operating Base Prince."

"You mean the base formerly known as Prince," said the quick-witted voice. "Now it is known as FEMA Camp #3, though FEMA has nothing to do with it. All these camps are privately run by PCRC contractors. They have told the country that the infected are being housed on college campuses until a cure can be found and administered. You and I both know there is no cure."

"So...what are they housing them for?"

"For de-pop," came the cryptic response. "De-population. Just like if they were bird flu-stricken poultry."

The camera switched and displayed a shot of hundreds of Skells being herded into the large white buildings erected on the quad by men in hazmat suits. Once the infected were inside, the doors were sealed, and those same men picked up large tubes that were connected to the tanker trucks. They inserted the nozzles into portals on the side of the building and began pumping something into the facility.

The picture on Woodrow's computer changed to a view from the inside of the building. The feed looked down from a camera mounted on the ceiling. White foam was being pumped in. It filled the room and as foam submerged the Skells, they convulsed and struggled. They thrashed and howled and screeched and clawed at themselves and each other until they were finally still. It was a gruesome death, even for those that already seemed to be dead.

"That is fire retardant foam," the cow head said. "It sucks all the oxygen from the room. It envelops their bodies and suffocates the infected. They are then carted off for incineration in special ovens that had been created to cremate livestock without causing smell or soot. Do you know how long it takes to incinerate an entire cow? Eight hours. It takes eight hours to completely incinerate a single cow. There's your Jeopardy question for the day."

"I can't believe they're doing this," Woodrow began with a shout, but when he realized he wasn't alone in the house, he toned it down.

"Well, they are. The infected are treated as if they're already dead. As if they no longer matter. To us, they matter. We don't fully understand what these people have become, but even if they are the walking dead, dead lives matter."

Woodrow looked away from the horrific events on the screen.

The voice continued: "You will let the world know what is happening and you will be their voice. You will let the world know who made them and who is destroying them."

"I'm sorry... I...just can't." Woodrow's voice faded into a whisper. "I have done enough damage."

"May we show you one more thing? Perhaps this will incentivize you," the voice said.

The camera switched again and there was a live feed of Fiona, she was sitting in front of her computer, and was taken very much by surprise when Woodrow appeared on her own screen as well.

"Woodrow?!" She yelled with a smile—startled, but happy.

"Fiona!" He replied

"How are you doing this?" She asked, looking around her laptop as if he could be hiding behind it.

The electronic voice interrupted the reunion. "Thirty seconds, Dr. Woody."

"What is going on?" Fiona asked. "How did you contact me?"

"Fiona, listen to me, I did not do this. Some cyber group has hacked our systems and wants to show me how they can get to you."

The voice continued the countdown. "Twenty seconds, Dr. Woody."

"Is that someone with you? Where are you? I want to see you," she said.

"No, they're not with me. You can't come see me. I was hiding out at Princeton University when it all went crazy. I am just outside campus right now, and I am safe." Woodrow pleaded. "You need to stay out of New Jersey."

"I'm already here! Mr. Gold flew me in on his jet. I'm here in Cape May."

The voice: "Ten seconds, Dr. Woody."

Woodrow furrowed at the screen. "Listen Fiona, please stay safe, I need to take care of something, it will explain everything in time, but please believe me, it will..."

"One second left."

Fiona and Woodrow each reached forward and touched their respective computer screens.

The screens went blank.

Woodrow's display changed back to the man in the rubber cow head. "That was nice."

"Go to hell," Woodrow snapped, his eyes welling with tears.

"I will assume you have agreed our arrangement," the voice said smugly. "By the way, while you were having that little reunion with your girlfriend, we tapped into another laptop in the house you are occupying. Seems your tubby security guard friend also found a laptop in the house."

The screen showed a video streaming live from Smoothie's laptop. He was sitting in what appeared to be a home office inside the same house, and he was staring intently at whatever was on his screen, oblivious that he was being viewed in real time.

The voice said, "Can you believe this guy got online and did not attempt to view one single news site? No CNN, no Whitehouse.gov. All this guy has done since he accessed the web is view porn. He didn't even try to check email. Just porn, porn, porn. Perhaps this country deserves what's happening to it."

Smoothie stood up and started to unbuckle his pants.

"Whoa!" The voice said and the screen switched back to the rubber cow head. "That would be something we couldn't un-see." The rubber cow head turned its attention back to Woodrow. "So, Dr. Woody, find the Colonel's laptop, turn it on, and double-click the icon marked 'Broadcast.' It will start broadcasting the laptop's webcam to all major news networks and websites. Once you hit it, we will also have access to his system, and we will stream the video from the FEMA camps' security cameras. You can tell the world whatever you want, as you too will be broadcasting. Tell them what they are seeing, and how the virus will soon be unleashed around the country, so that the PCRC will have to come in and take over their states as well. We expose them, and then we will leave you and your girlfriend to live happily ever after."

Woodrow did not respond. He let out a sigh and hung his head, nodding it slightly to acknowledge the voice.

While not visible, Woodrow had a feeling the person in the cow head was smiling. "Start the movement, spread the word, be the spark, the influencer you always wanted to be. Just get that damn laptop. You have until midnight."

12

SKELFIES

Dr. Zed here with your Infected Update Report.

The social media app FaceChat found itself in the middle of a fight between free speech and human decency.

We have seen planking, owling, and Tebowing. Well now, the new *meme* that has been taking over social media has become *Skelfies*. Skelfies are selfies taken by individuals posing with the most horrific looking Skell they could find.

Plenty of people found this act abhorrent. FaceChat removed the posts and threatened action against future postings of Skelfies, citing their end user licensing agreement, which forbids posting photos of dead bodies.

This decision led to a massive blowback from free speech advocates, who stated that there has been no determination that the Skells are, in fact, dead, and the official government stance is that these are infected peoples.

Others said that if users were forbidden to post these pictures, then would it be a violation to post pictures of family members who are suffering from terminal cancer and AIDS? If Skells are simply people afflicted with a disease, then there should be no ban on posting pictures with them.

FaceChat public relations floated the idea that posting photos of infected family members could be allowed, being the infected is a blood relative or spouse. The tech company and their community came to an agreement where photos of uninfected with Skells can be posted provided they do not show bare female breasts or imagery that could be considered insensitive to "protected groups."

What has been banned are photos and videos of "Skelfie Fails," which are pictures and photos of people who attempted to take a Skelfie, only to find the infected was not as docile as they anticipated, and were bitten, killed, or consumed as a result of these actions.

Even for the internet, that's just a bit much.

13
CONVERSATIONS FROM THE BEGINNING OF THE END

Dr. Woodrow Coleman walked past the lounging soldiers who had made themselves at home and spread themselves out about the house. Some played video games they had found, others flipped through magazines or seemed lost in thought. A few had positioned themselves at the windows, serving as lookouts. In the other houses on the cul-de-sac were more soldiers who had followed the colonel. They were lounging around as well, waiting for his next command, his next move.

Woodrow found Colonel Tindall sitting alone at the table in the formal dining room of the house. Tindall was flipping through the small bible he always carried with him in his uniform pocket.

"Colonel Tindall, what are your plans?" Woodrow asked.

"Only God has a plan for us," was the disinterested response. He may as well have said, "How the hell should I know."

"Ooookaaayy, but what do *you* plan to do?" Woodrow rephrased the question. "We can't all stay in this house forever. Eventually, either the authorities will find us, or the family will come home."

"Do you believe this is judgment day, son?" the colonel asked, taking the conversation in a different direction.

Woodrow gave a weak laugh. "No, I don't believe God or judgment have anything to do with this. I know this is a virus. A bad one, but no different than SARS, or Bird Flu or AIDS, and it will be tackled and cured."

Col. Tindall locked his eyes onto Woodrow's. "My little girl is with my sister right now. I got her out of the state in time. My wife had been bitten when we stopped for gas on the way. Once she was bitten, she knew what was going to happen to her. As soon as we made it out of state, we said our goodbyes to our daughter, as my wife had chosen to come back with me, in case I could find a so-called cure."

Woodrow tried to comfort the soldier. "We will find a cure, sir."

Tindall shot back: "How do you find a cure for death?"

"Well, death is a complex issue, finding a cure for death would be like creating a new form of life. I don't believe it is our role to create life."

73

Tindall said, "Maybe we already have. Maybe these things *are* a new form of life. Life different than we know it."

Woodrow stayed silent, not sure where this conversation was going.

Tindall frowned. "My daughter has Batten Disease. Do you know what that is?"

Woodrow had studied the brain-disintegrating sickness in college. "I do."

"She will not live to see her next birthday."

Woodrow looked to his feet. "Sir, I am sorry to hear that."

"She's dead, she doesn't know it yet, but she is. She's still walking around, just like these freaks out on the street. What is the difference between them and her?"

Woodrow stood silent.

Tindall sniffed. Exasperation on his face. "What do you want Dr. Coleman? Why are you here?"

Woodrow said, "I believe I can fix this. I believe that for even those who we can't cure, they should still be treated humanely. I know what the PCRC are doing to these things, these people. I know they are not housing them for a cure. They are exterminating them. Suffocating them, dismembering them, and incinerating them, all while the public thinks their loved ones they are being cared for until a cure is found."

Tindall shrugged. "Very little I can do about that right now."

"All I need is your government laptop and I can expose this. You would not want your daughter or your wife treated this way. Let me expose this so we can put a stop to it."

Tindall reached into his rucksack on the ground and retrieved the rugged laptop. "I was planning on destroying it anyway. As soon as I turn it on, it can be tracked, so it's no good to me. I am taking my remaining men. I know of some property where we can all hole up, regroup, and figure out our next steps. You can come with me if you want, as well as your two friends. But I am not telling you where we are going, so you have to make your choice now. Once we leave, if you stay behind, you're on your own—you won't see us again."

"Thank you, sir, I will leave it to Moz and Jack if they want to go with you, but I can't. I have someone I need to find."

Colonel Tindall nodded. "You need to wait at least one hour after I leave before you turn on that laptop. Once you turn it on, you will be located, and the PCRC forces will be here in minutes. You'll probably be arrested."

Woodrow returned the nod. "That's okay, I have some friends in high places. I need to get to them anyway, and this is the fastest way to make that happen. Oh, and colonel, one last thing: I need you to provide any password I need to access the laptop."

"Number one, Jesus saves."

"Um, that's fine, sir, but as I was asking—"

"That is my password, the number one, followed by Jesussaves, as one word, with a capital J. I don't mind sharing it with you. I won't be using that password again."

14
GO FETCH

Following Mr. Spencer's departure from President Callahan's office, Patrick and Daniel sat in silence for what felt like an eternity. Daniel looked at Patrick, Patrick looked at the closed door that Spencer and Dr. Reynolds just exited through as if he were trying to remotely view the man as he entered Maxwell Gold's office. Would his briefing to Maxwell be identical as the one had had just given to the president? Patrick would like to be a fly on the wall, or at least have some sort of listening device hidden in Maxwell's desk.

Patrick was experiencing more thoughts like these. He assured himself that it's not really paranoia if they truly are out to get you.

As if a switch was flipped, Patrick returned to his body and focused on Daniel. "I'm glad you're here," he said. "I'm glad you're alive. We lost a lot of people."

Daniel looked around at the surrounding phalanx of guards. "Can we have some privacy?"

"Unfortunately, no. They never leave me. They're like gun-toting herpes."

Daniel sneered a little. "They working for Max?"

"We all work for Max now. *All* of us," Patrick responded. He implied that "all" meant everyone beyond those in the room, and perhaps those in the building. "Besides, they just heard me get briefed on the zombie apocalypse and the dismantling of the United States, physically and figuratively. So there is nothing you and I have to discuss that's worse than that."

"You wear the crown now, pal," Daniel said with a small frown.

"Things are moving quickly. Yesterday, I signed an urgent needs contract with the PCRC to handle all security efforts during stability operations here in New Jersey. They will be handling everything from rubble removal to law enforcement to refugee management."

"Where's your family?"

Patrick's weak smile went away. "They're safe, they're out of state, in an undisclosed location, and under...twenty-four-hour observation." His words hinted that the guard was not necessarily for their protection, but possibly to ensure his obedience. "Speaking of family, your brother James was in here earlier today."

Daniel's response was fast and vicious: "Fuck him, that asshole!"

Patrick's smile returned. "He had the same thing to say about you. I guess it runs in the family."

"If I ever see him again, I'm putting a bullet in his head," Daniel said, standing up from his chair.

"You and I both know that's not going to happen. You Sullivans have to stick together, no one else can handle being around all of you."

Daniel growled. "Bullshit! This isn't some fight over a girl. Our brother's dead and it's his fault."

"I heard about Gerald, I'm truly sorry. But Jimmy had nothing to do with that. Neither did Max. Jimmy was devastated. It really messed him up when he heard. He's broken, and I don't know if there is a fix. He's a guy who's been through a lot, seen a lot of death. Losing Gerald seemed to put him over the edge. We flew Fiona in and he's staying with her here in the hotel, or uh... Whatever you call this place now."

Daniel leaned forward in his chair. "So who were they?"

"Those guys who went to collect Ivan were not working for Max," Patrick assured.

"Then who?" Daniel countered. "If they weren't working for the corporation, who the hell were they working for?"

"The competition," Patrick responded in a matter of fact tone that rubbed Daniel the wrong way. "I know this is hard to get your mind around, but this was not much more than an industrial accident. Things were not supposed to go down like this. I don't know the full story, but I know what I've been told over the past two weeks or so, and while it seems crazy, I have no reason to believe it's a lie. I can't tell you much more. Not right now," Patrick said with a quick eye shift towards a phone on the desk.

Daniel realized that somebody within the corporation was probably listening in to this entire conversation. He knew Patrick's family was leverage, and no prodding or threatening was going to make Patrick spill the beans at the moment. "So why am I here, *Mr.* President?" Daniel said with a condescending tone.

"Because we have some loose ends. Ivan is still out there and we need to either find him, or find what remains of him. The competition is still looking for him. Max needs to know that he's safe."

"Safe, or dead? Christ, Max really is father of the year." Daniel scoffed. "No wonder Ivan dug a hole in the ground to live in." Daniel leaned back and relaxed, as he knew this was going to be a simple tracking job. He had moonlighted as a bounty hunter before to make extra money. It was a job he was comfortable with.

Daniel continued: "Do you have any leads on his whereabouts. Last I saw him, he was hunkered down in that house out in Morristown."

"He torched that place," Patrick said, shaking his head. "Who knows where he is now. Maybe holed up in another one of his custom bunkers, or he's been eaten and is being digested in an infected person's stomach. Or, knowing him, he could be in this very building in the room next door. But what we do know is that he hasn't gotten out of New Jersey since the quarantine. So, if he is alive, he is here. He is hiding, he is pissed, and he is dangerous. Max is not going to rest till he knows where he is."

"Well, why don't you send some of these dogs out to hunt him?" Daniel said, motioning to 7322, who was still standing a few feet behind, still at parade rest.

"We need this done quick. You know Ivan and he trusts you. The situation in Jersey is pretty fragile. We're keeping it together the best we can, and we're trying to stop it from spreading outside our region."

Daniel crossed his arms. "So if Max is running the show here, what the hell do you do as president?"

"I *am* the president, *Daniel*. That is the chain of command, and no matter how this came about, I am the rightful and sworn leader of this country right now. What am I doing? I've been on the phone with world leaders for the past forty-eight hours. I spoke to the goddamn Vatican twice. They believe this is the sign of end times. I had to explain to them that this is being resolved and it's a viral outbreak, no different than Ebola. All I need is the Pope going out there and announcing the apocalypse and then I have a Jonestown massacre on a global level."

Talk about drinking the Kool-Aid, Daniel thought.

"Meanwhile," Patrick said, "I have governors asking what I'm going to do to protect their states and to stop this outbreak from spreading, from crossing state borders. I have thousands of people wanting to flee New Jersey, and almost as many others outside that are demanding entry back in. So, Danny boy, please, can I ask you to take one thing off my plate? Please go get Ivan, and if he is alive, please keep him that way. Could you do that for me?" Patrick smiled, a real smile this time. "As your Commander in Chief."

Daniel nodded. "You got it, chief."

"Thank you. One last thing: the old man wants to see you, give you a send-off. 7322 will take you to his office."

15
THE SULLIVAN THEORY OF EVERYTHING

The Sullivan family resembled a micro-universe, a cluster of planets, each trapped in the gravitational pull of the others. They could not escape; the gravity was too strong, no matter how hard they strained against its invisible bonds. The siblings—three brothers and one sister—were constantly at war with each other. Allegiances between them shifted—allies today could be combatants tomorrow. But, still, they always were within each other's orbit. Even when one brother would declare his absolute hatred for and permanent dismissal of the rest of the family, you could ask him at any given time what each of the other siblings was up to and he would instinctively know. They were always in each other's personal affairs.

They had worked out unique communication protocol. If Sibling A was not talking to Sibling B, they knew they could get a message to that sibling by sharing what they wanted to say with either Sibling C or Sibling D. This type of subterfuge became the main source of interpersonal communication between them.

Even when their sainted, long-suffering mother died, the bond was not broken. It had been Gerald who stepped in and became the center of the twisted Sullivan universe. Once order was restored, their life, and fights, and forgiveness, and more fights, continued on.

Now Gerald was dead, and the bonds seemed to have finally been snapped. Nature abhors a vacuum, and the death of Gerald had created chaos in their universe, sending the planets spiraling off into the abyss. History demonstrates that everything eventually collapses. Buildings, societies, and even the universe, will eventually collapse.

16

FOAMING

Mr. Spencer turned a page in his folder to move on to the next topic of his briefing to Mr. Gold. "As for the confirmed outbreaks, we have just begun the process of infected depopulation, or DEPOP, as it's referred to. As you are well aware, the most effective way to put them down quickly and permanently is to disembowel them. This is a slow, manual, and rather gory method. Also, the public believes that the infected, including the family members they turn over, are being housed and cared for in the universities and colleges around the state that we seized. We need to ensure that our eradication plans and processes are kept secret. We need the public's complete support if we are to identify and remove the Skells.

"The infected need oxygen, but we found that we need to inflict full body immersion in order for suffocation to be complete. An infected individual who has survived for several days, allowing the infection to work its magic on the human body, can actually reach a state where they can exist without a head. Oxygen is being absorbed somehow even when there is no mouth or throat evident. We believe that they have adapted to absorb oxygen through the skin, which allows them to keep moving, even with the head removed. So that leaves us with two effective methods: drowning or foaming."

Mr. Spencer turned another page in his binder. He kept talking.

"Drowning is not a viable option for the large scale disposal effort we need to undertake. We were utilizing the indoor pools at several recreation centers and universities, but the bodies, as are all bodies, prove to be buoyant, and thus, there is no easy way to keep them down long enough to terminate. The only water source large enough to support the sheer volume of infected is to force them into the Atlantic, but this is a nonstarter.

"First, there would be no way to herd such a large amount of infected into the ocean without the possibility of people seeing the activity. Next, we would need to then fish out all the drowned corpses, some of which could get swept away with the tide. Finally, it would affect seafood source and pollutes the water tables."

"You seem to have really thought this through," Maxwell said with concern.

"Thank you, sir." Spencer smiled, not realizing he was being looked at like a psychopath. "So that leaves us with foaming."

Maxwell raised an eyebrow. "Foaming?"

Spencer knew this was going to be a difficult discussion, but he needed to keep it as unemotional and clinical as possible. "Foaming is the most effective and humane way to deal with the poultry population during the avian flu outbreak. We herd the infected individuals into warehouses and fill the facility with water-based foam. The same foam that is used by fire departments for suppression of forest fires can be used very effectively, inexpensively, and humanely to carry out depop. The foam prevents oxygen from reaching the infected host body. The state has a large quantity of it and we have additional shipments coming in from the West Coast. They store silos of the stuff for wildland fires."

"Jesus Christ," Maxwell snapped. "This sounds like something right out of the Third Reich here. Why don't we just put them into gas chambers?"

"Sir, in this situation, nothing is off the table. But building gas chambers the size of warehouses would take months. Besides, we have no access to Zyklon B, or any similar kind of chemical. And, even if we did, we would need to have trained hazmat people on staff just to handle it.

"The foam is biodegradable, so it is not harmful to the environment. Also, we can utilize existing structures. We have warehouses being utilized right now, and more depopulation facilities are being erected as temporary structures in FEMA camps. We funnel the infected into the facilities, fill with foam to a height of seven feet, wait thirty minutes, and then clean the facility out with bulldozers. The remains are considered a biohazard, and so will be disposed of accordingly."

"Well, at least we're committing eco-friendly genocide," Maxwell said with venom.

Mr. Spencer took a deep breath. "We need to increase the scope and speed of depop. The infected are like walking virus distribution systems. Simple containment of the infected was determined to not be a viable solution, as the infected are just too dangerous. The transmission rate appears to be increasing exponentially and we have not even begun the work on a cure, if any exists. We need to eradicate the virus, meaning removing the transportation and distribution systems of the virus, which means eradicating the people infected."

Mr. Spencer waited for a response from Maxwell. Anger, denial, or indignant refusal to accept the circumstances.

He received no such pushback, so he continued.

"We need to practice good bio-surveillance and rapidly eliminate new outbreaks as they occur. We are ground zero of what is on the cusp of becoming a national epidemic, perhaps global, if we fail to nip it in the bud. Once you sign this order, we will expand to statewide depopulation and processing of the infected, as will our contractors and facilities we have on standby in other states that currently are, or may soon be, experiencing outbreaks.

"This plan will not be shared with anyone outside our company and all involved have been vetted to ensure their understanding of the need for secrecy, at least at this point. Not even the president is aware of this program. I know what we have to implement here is difficult to stomach..." Spencer realized what he just said the second he said it, and he hoped that Maxwell did not think he was intentionally making a joke of the whole stomach turning into a brain side effect.

No such rebuke occurred.

Mr. Spencer said, "We need to get in front of this and we only have a brief window." He laid the folder containing the order to move forward in front of Maxwell. He picked up a pen and placed it on top of the document.

Maxwell moved slowly. He gripped the pen. He had signed many documents during his career. When his company was awarded large contracts from the government worth millions of dollars, Maxwell would make a big show of signing the contract, and would use four or five pricy Waterford pens that would then be handed out to those who made the project or deal possible.

The pen he held in his hand now was cheap, plastic, and said The Congress Hotel, Cape May, NJ. It was one of thousands of identical pens produced. And it was about to sign a document that would result in the extermination of thousands of Americans.

Maxwell signed the document and closed the folder.

Spencer picked up the folder and held it to his chest as if he feared the signer might leap from his seat and rip it away. "Thank you, sir. You have done what is best for the country, perhaps the world. Now, we need to discuss the GRASS issue."

17
EGOS AND SILOS

"The domestic situation here in the continental US can best be described as bi-polar," Mr. Spencer said, his eyes on Maxwell Gold. "While there have only been sporadic outbreaks and unrest around the country, the vast majority of the public shrugged it off. We have not confirmed to the media that Texas has indeed declared secession from the rest of the country, but we have created uncertainty about why we have dispatched the National Guard down there.

"We have channeled information to selected media sources that the cause of the Skell virus was due to the mass influx of immigrants from South and Central America. We fed them quotes from overwhelmed Department of Homeland Security and Customs and Border Protection personnel stating that due to the sheer number of border crossings, they just could not provide the proper medical screenings. But we fed other sources that it was most likely caused by a bio-terror attack from the Middle East. So as usual, the public does not know what the hell to think.

"California is the next problem. Much of their unrest is self-inflicted, but then again, when have California's problems not been self-created. They are the drama queen of the fifty states." He smiled.

Maxwell's face was stone.

It was a terrible attempt at humor. Spencer had picked the wrong audience.

He cleared his throat and said, "We have a real situation unfolding with the GRASS movement. I have not had the chance to brief President Callahan on this matter. Perhaps it would be a breach of protocol for me to brief a national security issue with you before I discuss it with him, or perhaps I could brief you two together?"

Maxwell, clearly irritated, snapped at Mr. Spencer. "Cut the crap, you and I both know who you report to. I will tell you what you will and won't brief to the president. Patrick is to be told nothing of what we just discussed, such as the false flag cover stories we are floating. This is to never reach his desk. Is that understood?"

Spencer was sweating. "Yes, sir. Don't worry, we have so many false stories out there that we have plausible deniability for anything. Everyone with an ego wants to feel like they have the inside scoop, yet every agency is in their own silo, so information is never shared."

Maxwell glared at Spencer.

Spencer gave him a nervous smile. "Well, except you, sir. You are completely in the loop of all information."

Maxwell discontinued his death glare.

Spencer continued cautiously. "But in honesty, we don't need to communicate that much. We have placed like-minded people in key roles. They don't need to be told what to do, they understand what needs to be done."

Maxwell said, "I understand. Now go ahead and tell me about these GRASS assholes."

Spencer bent down and pulled a larger folder from his briefcase. "The precursors of the movement can be traced back to two individuals. Ronan Campbell, age 30, raised in a rural area of Hayden, Idaho. Founder of a punk rock band out of San Francisco called Roman Kandle. His shtick is spouting Nazi propaganda disguised as social justice. He hooked up with Majesty Steinman, some spoiled east coast princess who reinvented herself as a radical animal rights activist and militant vegan while attending the University of California at Berkeley. She used social media, as well as her parents' unlimited funding, to grow a pretty large following under the banner Green Rights Action.

"Obviously, this guy's Aryan leaning did not extend below his belt, as Mr. Campbell happily hooked up with Ms. Steinman.

"Majesty and Ronan are two bad tastes that taste worse together. Web and social media savvy, they grew their flock online. They were accused of, but never proven to have committed, multiple fire bombings of steak house restaurants and fast food joints where beef or chicken was the staple food. They had also vandalized farms, setting animals and poultry free. As their message and movement crystallized, more serious acts of violence followed. Green Rights Action Schutzstaffel became GRASS, and those that came out to jeer their protests were set upon by supporters, beaten, kicked, spit upon, and splattered with animal blood. We believe they received a lot of outside funding and support from foreign anti-American entities who saw them as useful idiots—a means to hurt a common enemy. It was truly astonishing how fast things got out of control, and before anyone knew it, they had multiple footholds in California. Areas became law enforcement no-go zones and within months. The state has fallen pretty much to their control."

Maxwell sat back in his chair, moving his jaw back and forth as if he was chewing something over. "I see." Maxwell saw opportunity.

18
BLISTERS

Gary Ragu had a difficult choice. His entire life had been pulled out from under him like a cheap rug. The man he had worked for, served and obeyed, even killed for, was a fraud and a snitch. Big V had turned state's witness and was working as a rat for the FBI. In fact, his betrayal may have caused this entire zombie outbreak.

Ragu was faced with the choice between turning rat for Agent Schaffer to ensure the safety of himself and his remaining crew, or turn to the other mob capos and plead his case in the hope that they didn't kill him on sight. He would have to tell them that he knew nothing of V's betrayal. Even if he did succeed in earning, or at least buying, his way back into the mob's good graces, he and his crew would still be stuck in Jersey. His fate could be to end up being chewed to mush in the stomach of a zombie or cut up into pieces and placed in garbage bags scattered throughout the Meadowlands. *Either manner of death,* he thought, *would be better than life in a federal penitentiary.* He would take his chances with the mob capos.

Ragu had a fighter's background. One of nine kids born to old school Italian American parents whose parenting skills could have been picked up from *Lord of the Flies.* Growing up, the brothers had to fight for their parents' attention, approval, and even for what food was in the house.

Sunday dinners were at a decibel level that rivaled Newark Airport. Once, it was revealed during a meal that Ragu had lost a fight at school. The father slammed his fists on the table and yelled: "Gary, this better not be true, don't embarrass me, don't embarrass me!"

Later that night, his old man dragged Gary to the other boy's house to make them fight again.

He escaped this brood when he was recruited into a more stable, and in some aspects, less violent, family: the Jersey mob. He started out as a street hood, but soon rose the ranks and became Big V's right hand man. He and V bonded when not long after Big V's father was whacked, Ragu's father also was taken out over some drunken words exchanged in a bar. Neither killer was ever identified or apprehended.

Ragu would go to the mob enclave and plead his case. First, he needed to know where the meeting was being held and he needed someone to bring him in that was a trusted yet neutral party.

Dominic "Dom" Dispensa was known as a neutral. He was so neutral, and bland, and non-threatening, that even his nickname was dull. He was in the bloodline of once respected mob boss Big Lou Dispensa, Sr., and he was the nephew of the reviled boss Louis Dispensa Jr.

"You came to the right guy, as right now, looks like I'm the last man standing," Dominic said to Ragu. "No need for you to go to the Pine Barrens, nothing left of those guys other than a mess on the floor resembling beefaroni. When the bosses didn't return, we assumed the worst. Maybe it was an FBI sting. Or one of the bosses pulled a power play. Seen it before, call for a sit-down as a set-up to whack the other bosses. We went up there to find out what was going on, and the place looked like the killing floor of a slaughterhouse. What a horror show."

"Anyone make it out alive?" Ragu asked.

"Don't know. It was such a mess up there, who knows if they were in the pile or not. Our guys torched the cabin and we left."

"Have you heard from out of state?"

"I have," Dominic proclaimed. "Word's come down. For now, I'm in charge and you're number two."

Ragu threw a white box of pharmaceuticals onto the desk and plopped down into the leather chair in front of Dom's desk. "A tribute," he said.

Dom picked up the package and began opening it.

Ragu explained his gift. "Twenty-two blister packets of Adderall, something to help ease the mind of he who wears the crown."

Dominic physically cringed. "Please, don't say that word."

"Adderall?" Ragu asked.

"No, blister. God, I hate that word," Dom said, still uncomfortable while working a couple pills from their packets.

"I hear ya," Ragu commiserated. "I hate the word aluminum. I can never say that friggin word. Al...oom...a...num," Ragu said sounding out the word phonetically.

"It's not that I can't say it, it's just when I hear that word, I think of little white blisters that appear on your dick." Dom crossed his legs.

"Um. Do... Do you have blisters on your dick?"

"No!" Dominic said defensively. "Just makes me think of that. *Shit.*"

Ragu had an endless parade of ball-busting comments lined up in his mind, but as this moron in front of him was now the boss, he kept them to himself. He would be sure to share with Vito and Vitamin Mike later.

"So listen, Ragu, you and I both know I don't want this honor that has befallen to me. I'm not interested in running this family. I know you are. I can't just give it to you though, even we have rules, and there are people above me, people from out of state, that would not look too kindly on my handing the reigns to you. It could be perceived as a sign of weakness. Weakness creates challengers."

"I understand," Ragu said.

Dom arched his eyebrows. "But if you could prove yourself..."

"What the fuck you want me to do, pull a sword from a stone or something?"

"No, I need you to kill your old boss. Big V."

Ragu sat forward in the chair. "I thought he was dead, or out of state, under witness protection or something?"

"Nope, he's alive, and he's right here in South Jersey. He was spotted in Cape May this morning. Find him, kill him, bring me indisputable proof he's dead, and the crown is yours. You would be the sole Don running Jersey, at least till we rebuild the family."

19

ONE LAST FAVOR

Daniel left his meeting with Patrick and proceeded on down the hallway for his meeting with Maxwell.

7322 followed closely behind.

Men and women walked hurriedly down the halls, papers and binders in hand, some barked into cell phones.

They approached a door about five rooms down from Patrick's Oval Office. It had two guards in black uniforms standing on either side, one a tough looking man, the other a tough looking yet thoroughly attractive woman.

7322 seemed to know her. She wore the identifier of 9104.

"He's been expecting you, to go right in," 9104 said with an ominous tone.

While reaching for the door, 7322 hesitated. A subconscious action that was noticed by both Daniel and 9104.

"Don't worry." 9104 smirked. "We fed him already."

7322 gave her a "Go fuck yourself" glance, but he was clearly embarrassed by his own subconscious hesitation. He opened the door, let Daniel walk in first, followed him inside, and closed the door behind them.

Daniel scanned the room. It probably was the office of hotel management less than two weeks ago. It was unimpressive, with a single desk, phone, fax machine, and some file boxes. Any personal items from the previous occupant had been removed. There was no opulence in the room now serving as the seat of power of the country. It had the tools for function, nothing more. There were no guards standing inside this office to protect or monitor Gold.

Something else was missing, too: James.

For as long as Daniel could remember, he had never seen Maxwell without his brother James being right at the old man's side.

Daniel walked towards Maxwell's desk. He felt none of the hesitancy that his escort 7322 had felt. After all, he had known Maxwell for his entire life. He *thought* he knew him, anyway.

Daniel sat down in the chair in front of the desk. 7322 stayed behind with his back to the closed door.

"So, first I met with the president," Daniel said, "and now I meet with you. Whose office do I go into next, Jesus Christ's?"

Maxwell's eyebrows bounced on his brow. "Oh, come on, Daniel, you don't believe stories about people who have risen from the dead, do you?"

Maxwell turned his head to look at 7322 and craned his neck as if he is attempting to read the label on his chest.

7322 stepped forward quickly. "Yes, sir, um, 7322." He pointed at his nametag.

"7322, could you please excuse us." It wasn't a question.

7322's face sunk a little. Like he did not know if he should feel rejection or relief. "Uh, sir?"

"It's all right, Mr. Sullivan and I have some catching up to do."

Daniel turned in his seat and gave 7322 a smirk to rub some extra salt in the dismissed man's wounds.

7322 turned and left.

Daniel refocused on Maxwell. "Patrick said you want me to go fetch Ivan for you."

"That's what I wanted him to think you're doing, and that is what he will continue to believe until there is a need for him to know otherwise. Daniel, it's time you were brought in from the dark. I need someone I can trust. I need a new Sullivan."

"So that's it? You get one brother killed, you turn the other into a basket case, and you think I'll just step in and fill the gap."

"I'm sorry about your brother, but this is the life we have chosen."

Daniel pointed an accusatory finger at Maxwell. "Bullshit. I did *not* choose it. It chose me. You chose me. I have not had freedom of choice for my entire life."

Maxwell sighed. "You always had a choice. You can choose to walk out that door right now. This is not a prison. It's still a free country, and will remain so as long as I have a say."

"You? I thought Patrick was the new leader of the free world?"

"Daniel, are you in or out," Maxwell demanded.

"I'm out." Daniel stood up and walked towards the door.

"Daniel, wait." The old man's voice seemed surprisingly consolatory, almost fatherly. "No more lies, no more obfuscation. It is time you were brought in. If you stay, if you help me, I will tell you everything."

Daniel stopped.

Maxwell rose from his seat. "This is bigger than you, bigger than New Jersey. This is the beginning of a new nation. There's no going back now. We have set off a chain of events that can only move forward. But I need you more than ever before. I need your help now. And I promise, I will tell you everything."

Daniel turned and walked back to the chair and sat down.

"Everything," he said.

20
REPO MEN

Daniel left Maxwell's office to find 7322 waiting just outside the door. The soldier had been chatting with 9104, but they both ceased mid conversation the second the door opened.

Daniel gave each a "what's up with you two" glance. He turned towards 7322. "Max is sending us out on a search and recover mission to find some damn truck. He said you would fill me in."

When 7322 didn't answer, Daniel pushed. "So, why the hell is he sending us out to pick up a goddamn truck?"

7322 crossed his arms. "Your friend Virgil was working for the feds."

Daniel shot back, "Bullshit."

"He was good at covering his tracks. Even Max was unaware of his arrangements. He was working as an informant and was looking to secure a good deal for himself and his family. Here is what we know: He was given the order by his FBI handlers to hijack a PCRC truck containing proprietary materials. We don't believe he knew or cared what was in them."

Daniel cocked an eye. "What was in there?"

"Frozen cuts of beef. It's from cattle raised and fed in a proprietary process that PCRC had spent tens of millions of dollars on in research and development. A process that the company's competitors would like to get a hold of. We believe a binder outlining the process was also in that truck. I don't know if Virgil got spooked or just did not want his fingerprints on this particular job because it was too close to Mr. Gold, but for whatever reason, he farmed out the actual hijacking job to a couple of Dispensa's guys. They grabbed the truck at a weigh station and scared off the driver.

"PCRC also has some well-placed informants in Dispensa's crew. The thugs that pulled off the heist did not know anything other than they were to steal a truck loaded with steaks and deliver it to a location in Maryland." 7322 shrugged. "Our guess is the hijackers got greedy, as the truck was never delivered. No honor among thieves. Once they opened the back and saw all those frozen high-end cuts of beef, they must have decided they could make more money by selling those steaks off to restaurants and butcher shops up and down the Garden State Parkway. Just hours after the truck had been stolen, the meat was being served and consumed by dozens of restaurants, hotels, and housewives.

"We need to find that truck and whatever contents are left in it. It represents tens of millions of dollars in corporate investment."

BMW walked up to join the group. He appeared freshly showered and shaved, and was wearing a brand new black tactical uniform matching the rest of the newly formed domestic security force. On his chest was the patch displaying his new moniker: 8080.

Daniel pulled BMW aside. He motioned with his hand up and down the outfit in disbelief as to what he was viewing. "Christ, this place is like invasion of the body snatchers, now they got you?"

BMW shook his head. "Nah man, but I've been wearing the same monkey suit from work for two days, I needed to change my drawers."

Daniel nodded towards the name, or rather number, tag. "That works out perfectly for you, 8080."

"Yeah, how's that?"

"8-0, looks like eight ball. The one black ball among all the other balls. Seems to be the story of your life."

BMW snarled "Man, fuck you, white boy."

Daniel smiled. Happy to lightly torment his friend. "Get it? Because eight balls are black, and you're black. You do know you're black right?"

"If we survive this, I'm gonna kill you."

"Not my fault you're black, not everyone can be blessed to be Irish."

The attractive 9104 approached them. "Mr. Sullivan, if you would like to follow me, we will get you fitted for your own uniform."

Daniel snorted. "Bullshit, I'm not wearing one of those."

BMW chimed in, "Oh, yes you are. You haven't changed your clothes since this shit started. You smell like sweat and ass, and you are not getting into my chopper stinking like that."

"Why don't you listen to your friend Mr. White," 7322 gently chided. "Or, perhaps I could call you 8080 now?"

Daniel corrected him. "You mean Eight Ball."

7322 was confused. "I thought you called him BMW?"

Daniel doubled down. "He's Eight Ball now."

7322 gave them both a perplexed look. "What the hell is it with you people and nicknames?"

Daniel shrugged. "It's a Jersey thing."

21
LAB PARTNERS

"What the fuck you looking at?"

Hardly a pleasant greeting for a refugee. Or perhaps, that was exactly the greeting most refugees received. Eric Pinskey was adjusting to his refugee status. Being one of the many minors whose parents were either trapped in NJ or killed in NJ, and with no other relative outside Jersey, he was an unaccompanied minor being managed by the state.

After escaping NJ and arriving on the shore of Delaware via mini-sub with Daniel Sullivan, along with Big V's daughter Rita, Eric had been handed off to one of Maxwell Gold's lackeys. Rita was turned over to the feds, as her father was a known mob boss and lesser-known FBI informant. Eric was shipped off to Virginia, which housed many of the orphaned and temporarily homeless children from the Garden State.

Minors were given a quick physical and a twenty-four-hour quarantine to ensure they had not been infected, then they were assigned foster homes and enrolled in school. As Eric was the only known survivor of Holy Friends Catholic School, he was sent off to a comparable institution Saint Bernadette's High School. His welcome there as a new sophomore was not much different than his welcome as a new freshman at Holy Friends.

"I said, what the fuck you looking at dickless?" came the repeated taunt from the upper classman.

"Nothing," was Eric's meek reply, not realizing he had just flung an insult.

"Damn right nothing," said the bully not realizing he had accepted the insult.

Eric felt the pang of loss. Not so much for his mother and step dad. He had no idea if they were alive or dead. His real father had been dead for years. He felt the loss of his core group of pals from Holy Friends. He did not make friends easily. He entered Holy Family the way he had left eighth grade: timid and beaten down by a lifetime of rejection. He was afraid to show any attention to any of the girls he had a crush on in school, since most girls were not satisfied simply rebuffing his interest—they had to ensure that it was known among the entire student body that some gross nerd had hit on them. They then had to publicly insult the boy every chance they got to ensure no one in the school was under any misperception that they would consider dating such a dweeb.

He craved popularity. He craved it like a Kardashian craved fame. Nothing else mattered. Academic achievements, straight A's, or even the rare acknowledgement from his parents were meaningless. He needed to achieve popularity like he needed oxygen. Yet it eluded him.

It was midway through the first year of high school when a new student entered the school. Eric got partnered with him for freshman biology.

"Chris Corcio. You can call me CC," he said, introducing himself to Eric.

Eric felt ashamed that he initially avoided hanging out with CC. He was the new kid and immediately became a target. But the way CC handled it was completely opposite to how Eric dealt with bullying. Eric absorbed every insult, every slight, every social failure like a sponge that was never squeezed or rinsed out. He carried the filthy residue inside him, which just made him even more unappealing.

CC was like a stone surface that shrugged it all off without anything sticking. He would try for girls way out of his league, and when they blew him off, he acted as if it was their loss. He seemed to relish their public taunts afterwards and gave it back twofold. When older or tougher kids tried to bully him, he busted their balls even worse, with no apparent fear of a courtyard beating after school.

He had confidence. He was not a looker, not tough, not athletic and not even that smart—but he dripped with confidence and it drew Eric in to learn this stranger's secret.

The two started hanging out together and CC later introduced Eric to other kids from school, some of whom were also freshman, but who Eric had never even met or noticed before. They were all pretty much loners until CC brought them together. He made Eric question why he desired to be accepted by those that he really did not like or care about. Why was it so important to him to be accepted and liked by jocks and mean girls at the school? He should, in fact, find self-assurance in the knowledge that he was not in the crowd of those who had everything: looks, popularity, athletic skill, but are such miserable assholes that they use their position to make those that have nothing feel even worse about their lives.

It was a liberating "come to Jesus" moment. Unfortunately, before he really had the time to take this new world view forward, the Skell virus hit and his school turned into a human buffet.

He heard a crash from down the hall and jumped. He was still shell-shocked from his last brush with death in NJ. He looked down the hall and two larger kids had thrown a freshman against some lockers. The kid was scooping up some cartoons he had drawn when Eric approached.

"Hey, here comes your girlfriend," the larger of the two said to the freshman.

"How would you even know what a girlfriend looked like?" Eric responded, not realizing he said it aloud till the words were out there.

"Hey pussy, I am going to kick your ass."

"How would you know what a pussy looked like if you never had a girlfriend?" Eric said, again, the words coming from somewhere beyond his capacity for bravery.

"You are *dead*. I am beating the shit out of you once school's over."

"I'll be done at three o'clock." Eric rocked on his heels. "What time does it end for you in special education?"

The freshman laughed.

"Y-y-y-your friggin dead!" the bully stammered before he and his friend walked off quickly.

Eric realized he was not dead. It was the first time he realized that since he left New Jersey. He helped the freshman up. "My name's Eric," he told the kid. "You can call me E."

22
EIGHT BALL CORNER POCKET

As Daniel was taken off by 9104 to shower and change, BMW and 7322 sat down in the cafeteria and chowed on breakfast. BMW had a plate of scrambled eggs and sausage. 7322 carried a mug of piping hot coffee.

7322 raised his mug to take a sip. "So, Mr. White, or may I now call you 8080?"

"You can call me BMW." He shoveled a forkful of eggs into his mouth.

7322 was still stuck on the nickname thing. "I thought that stood for Black Malcolm White, what the kids called you when you were in grade school. You don't find that a little offensive?"

"Not at all, I've made peace with it. I own it."

"Mr. White, we would like you to assist us on a project."

BMW stabbed a link of sausage and plopped it in his mouth. "Nah man, I'm not a mercenary like the Sullivan boys. I'm just a pilot."

"Well, that is a shame, because we need your piloting skills. We can ensure that you are compensated for your work with us."

"Thanks, but I really need to get back to Atlantic City. The chopper belongs to the casino. I don't want the law coming after me thinking I stole it."

"Mr. White, first of all, martial law has been declared and the local law enforcement now falls under the purview of the military, which currently falls under the purview of PCRC. So, your service and the casino's chopper is supporting the state's restoration operations."

"Understood," BMW insisted, "but still, I think it's time I was on my way."

"That is your choice, but your helicopter is staying here. We have a no-fly zone across New Jersey, so no civilian air travel is allowed. All non-approved flights will be forced down, or shot down."

"Look man, I'm not part of this," BMW said as he stood, abandoning his food.

"Everyone is part of this now," 7322 assured him. "There are no bystanders. If you want to leave, you are free to go. But you are not taking your helicopter. You can walk out of here, right now. The front door is just down that hallway. But I'm not sure how far you are going to get. You won't make it to Atlantic City on foot and I don't believe Uber is still running."

BMW sat back down. "If I help you, and when this is resolved, I can take my chopper and go?"

7322 took a friendlier tone. "I am not here to recruit you, but we are looking for good people. PCRC has the contract to provide security here in Jersey for the next three years. We will also be expanding to California to manage this terror upstart group GRASS. If the outbreak spreads beyond the state, we will expand the scope of our deployment."

BMW shrugged and began eating again. More eggs. "Well, when you put it that way, in the *Us vs Them* way, how could I say no? And if you get some sort of recruitment bonus for bringing me in, you better damn well split it with me."

Growing up one of the only black kids in an all-white suburb, he was regularly put in positions where he needed to make a choice of us vs them. Gangs from less lily-white neighborhoods approached him when he was out and about in high school. They also wanted him to make a decision, their gangs or a beating. He then managed to keep both sides thinking he was with them and against the others. He figured that, right now, it was time to do the same.

23
POST-TRAUMATIC CRAP SYNDROME

Daniel rejoined BMW and 7322 in the courtyard of the hotel. He had now been fitted with his own black tactical outfit and assigned the number 8150.

In the middle of the courtyard, two Skells were being held in a cage. They were pretty ravaged, seeming to have been infected for some time and having suffered the full effects of the virus. Bone thin, bulging stomach, eyes empty of any recognition, drooling, and hostile.

"We have been experimenting with some different types of less than lethal devices to help us manage and round up the infected," 7322 said, standing in front of a table with several devices displayed. "We do have some devices that will prove to immobilize the infected, while only causing temporary discomfort for the innocents around them."

Daniel eyed the gadgets on the table. "If these things are zombies, can't you just shoot them in the head?"

7322 grumbled. "First off, they're not zombies." Then he let out an exasperated sigh. "We don't have a complete understanding of the current situation, but I can tell you, these people are not reanimated corpses, they are infected living beings who need to be rounded up humanely, and placed into quarantine for their own protection, as well as for the public safety. FEMA has set up camps at the major universities around the state and we will be using the dorm rooms to house them until we can find a cure."

"Okay, so headshots are out," Daniel said.

"Well, actually, the infected are quite resilient, so we have had to resort to more unique methods. We found one of the most effective device is a modified free electron laser, which allow us to tune the frequency of targeted sound waves which affect the gastrointestinal processes of whomever it is directed at."

He removed the device from a plastic case the size of a footlocker. It looked like a parabolic microphone from the sidelines of football games. There was a handle at the bottom like a cordless drill and a foot-long silver rod with a plastic cone at the base.

7322 said, "This tool came from a classified Defense Threat Reduction Agency program called Thunder Storm. The project was experimenting with sonic weaponry. I will simplify this as much as I can, but they were experimenting with VLF's, or very low frequencies, that could create a resonance within human subjects."

BMW and Daniel stared at him blankly.

7322 continued: "Basically, all cells in your body are affected by electromagnetic vibrations. In fact, everything is vibrating all the time, at their own frequency."

Daniel played class clown. "Yeah, well, I'm vibrating off the ground right now just waiting to hear why the hell you're putting us through chemistry class."

"Well, it's actually more biology than chemistry."

Daniel started to walk away.

7322 called after him, "Okay, okay, let me get to the point. Resonance is when our device makes a connection with the target and both the device and the target cells begin vibrating at the same frequency. Once this link has been made, an energy exchange takes place in the membrane of each cell, causing a biological reaction. An enclosed chamber is usually needed to facilitate this resonance. For our purposes, we used the chamber of the stomach lining."

"You're killing me here, professor!" Daniel snapped in exasperation.

"No, keep going, this is interesting," BMW encouraged.

Daniel rolled his eyes. "Teacher's pet."

7322, obviously excited about what he was talking about even though his two students weren't, continued the lesson.

"What I am holding here is an ultrasonic generator, which emits a very low frequency directed towards the subjects, be they rioting citizens or flesh hungry Skells. The effects are not lethal, nor are they lasting, but they are nonetheless unpleasant. Nausea, vomiting, and incontinence are common. Now, with proper tuning and sound amplifiers, this device will greatly affect the stomach acid of the infected, causing them to become so confused as to be immobile. For those innocent bystanders who get caught in the burst, the effects are unpleasant, but nothing a little Pepto won't fix. But the worst reaction is ED."

BMW was confused. He shook his head. "ED? You mean like this?" He made a hand motion with his index finger bending downwards as if it was going limp.

7322 laughed. "Not *that* ED, I mean explosive diarrhea. That is why DTRA may have called this tool Thunder Storm, but we call it Shit Storm. They had designed it for non-lethal crowd control. It is pretty hard to riot when you've got a load in your pants."

He turned the device on. Other than a very slight hum, it did not appear to be working. He pointed the device at the Skells in the cage and pulled the trigger, causing them to immediately drop to the ground and convulse with seizures.

BMW squinted at the writhing monsters. "Why is it effecting them like that?"

7322 said, "That is classified, just know that it does work, and we will be bringing this into the field with us."

"Can I try that out?"

7322 handed him the gun but warned him not to point it at anyone other than the Skells.

0303 walked into the courtyard. "Well, well. Look what we have here, a young black male with a weapon. When I was a sheriff's deputy, I lived for such encounters." 0303 raised his arms in the air. "Hey partner, hands up don't shoot."

BMW pointed the device at 0303, smiled, and pulled the trigger.

0303 immediately dropped to a squatting position. One hand grabbed his stomach and the other his ass, as if he was trying to stop a garden hose. What emitted from him was a horrific sound and stench.

"I just shit my pants!" 0303 screamed. "What the hell happened, I just shit my fucking pants!"

7322 usually would not tolerate this type of action, but as BMW *was* the teacher's pet.

He let this particular infraction go.

24
LAWS OF GOD AND MAN

Brannagan was a hard man with a simple plan. Roll into town on his Harley, set up his kingdom in the bar of his choice, and let the citizens know that he would provide their protection—though it would come with a price. He would keep them safe from the zombie hordes as long as they met his every drunken, lustful whim. He would be a leader of violence and intimidation, of strength and severity. But over time, he knew that their fear would turn to respect, and then loyalty. That the women he would take would soon give themselves to him willingly. Wantonly. Those under his protection would grow to revere him as their savior, and when necessary, they would die for him.

He expected some would challenge his control of the town, and they would have to be dealt with harshly, brutally, fatally. He was ready. He had never taken a life before, but he was ready to do so to secure his place in this new, savage world of the Skells.

This was a now a place where strong men, men of action, ruled swaths of land. Town and camps of survivors would wage war with each other, conquering smaller groups to grow their ranks and power. He knew that his clan would look to him for protection from not only the infected, but from other men like him.

His mighty and embarrassing reign lasted 13 minutes.

His current throne was an uncomfortable steel chair bolted to the floor of the Bergen county jail.

The door opened and the guard escorted in a man in a very snappy suit and tie. "Here he is," the guard said to his well-dressed companion. "Your client, the Warlord of Weehawken." The guard let out a hearty laugh and left the two men to talk.

"Hello, Mr. Brannagan," said his court appointed lawyer. "My name is Ira Brillstein. I will be representing you at your hearing today. I want to ensure you understand the charges against you."

"What the fuck is going on here?" Brannagan said.

"Well, sir, you have been arrested and charged with assault. Would you like to tell me why you caused so much trouble at the Applebee's during lunch yesterday?" Ira spoke in a tone like he was talking to a troublesome child.

"Where the hell did those cops come from? We are in the middle of the fucking zombie apocalypse, and they arrested me for punching a goddamn bartender? There ain't no more law, man, this is the zombie apocalypse. End of days. People like me *are* the law now!"

"Weeeell, yes, there are zombies around," Ira reluctantly agreed. "Or at least reasonable approximations of zombies, if you desire to call these poor souls that. But this is not the apocalypse. Also, I believe the term 'zombie' refers to a reanimated dead person. These people are not that astonishing. They're just people with a bad virus, like the flu or AIDS."

Brannagan was still not coming to grips with the discrepancy between what he believed and what was occurring. "I saw it, man. On the TV. Zombies eating people. Cops and soldiers being overrun. This is the end. Let me out of this fucking jail!"

"Look." Ira's voice became soothing as he tried to calm his agitated client. "I know they say that only two things will survive the apocalypse, cockroaches and lawyers, but trust me, it just isn't happening yet." Ira's eyes flitted around the jail before returning to Brannagan's. "For example, tonight, I have dinner reservations with my wife and her mother. If this was the end of time, do you think that is how I would want to spend it?" He raised an eyebrow. "So, like it or not, life goes on. Later, I will be judged for my inadequacies, and tomorrow, you have an afternoon in court being judged for your mistakes."

Brannagan rested his head in his hands. "I... I thought it was all gone. I thought this was my time..." His voice trailed off. He was finally realizing the reality of his situation. He recalled entering the restaurant, of standing on the bar and announcing a self-appointed rule of the region. Then there was the laughter. The fight, the police, the handcuffs, and the very large amount of meth he had started the day with.

Ira smiled, still trying to calm and soothe. "Listen, Mr. Brannagan. You made a mistake. That's it. The bartender was not seriously harmed and most of the patrons thought it was a joke. There are bigger concerns on people's minds right now than a biker declaring himself king."

Brannagan seemed to wilt.

"So no, this is not the apocalypse," Ira said. "And yes, there is still law and in most places, order. I understand how confusing a time this is. I lived in Israel for two years. Did you know nearly everyone there carries guns? And not just pea shooters, I'm talking young men and women come in and lay down their assault rifles on the bar like it's an iPhone. Teachers are required to be armed when escorting children on field trips. Every time you get on a public bus, you wonder if it will blow up and if today will be the day you don't come home. But no one over there sees it as the apocalypse, and trust me, that is a region of people obsessed with end times."

Ira opened up his briefcase and took out his client's folder. "I suggest we plead guilty to simple assault and offer to pay damages to the restaurant. You will probably have to do some time, but no more than ninety days. Perhaps when you get out, this whole thing will have cleared up. But, if it does spiral out of control, you can try the whole road warrior thing again. Promise me you will make me Prince of Paramus, though, great mall there," his lawyer said with a smile.

Ira paused for a moment, lost in thought. Then he opened up the folder and laid it out before the man who would be king. "When the laws of god and man no longer apply, you and I will scarf down a ham and mayo on white bread while burning down my old high school gym teacher's house. How does that sound?"

25
FALSE IDOLS

Patrick grew weary of Mr. Spencer. This ever-present advisor was midway through his umpteenth briefing of the day. Something about some group that had begun worshiping the Skells, believing they have raised from the dead like Jesus, and there is concern of a mass suicide planned by the followers. Meanwhile, passing by Patrick's office door, the president observed generals, mayors, PCRC Security Forces Sector Leads, and businessmen as they made their way to and from meetings down the hallway with Maxwell Gold.

He had asked Maxwell about these meetings and why he was not involved.

"You have more pressing matters than to hear a lot of whining and questions you have already answered ten times. Leave the bullshit to me," was Maxwell's answer.

And yet, here he was, listening to a briefing about a bunch of fanatics who had forsaken their idols and decided to follow the infected, believing them raised from the dead.

"Okay, Spencer, what is your point? So a bunch of fanatics pray to the infected and may possibly want to commit mass suicide. Let them. It's still a free country. If they want to pray to space aliens and science fiction writers, they can do that as well. This hardly seems like a national security threat!" Patrick snapped at Spencer mid-sentence, startling the man.

Patrick frowned. "Who is Max meeting with now?"

Spencer fumbled with his papers. "Um, sir, I am not quite sure. I will have to check Mr. Gold's schedule."

"I want you to go down to his office right now and ask him to bring himself, and whomever he is meeting with at this moment, to my office so that I can sit in on the rest of the meeting," Patrick ordered.

"Mr. Gold has instructed us to never interrupt his meetings. Especially if the door is closed, he was—"

Patrick cut off the nervous sounding man. "I want you to go to his office and bring them down here." Patrick said, his voice becoming a low growl.

"Yes, sir, I will ask him—"

"What the fuck are you not understanding?" Patrick shouted, again cutting the man off. "I did not say *ask* him anything. I told *you* to *tell him* to cease his meeting and continue it in my office. Did you understand that, or do you need to clean the shit out of your ears?"

Spencer turned and walked out of the Oval Office in a hurry.

Patrick fiddled with the pens on his desk. He tried to calm down. He had lost it on Spencer, used language that didn't belong in the work environment. He was not used to handling situations, especially work situations, in such a manor. But he was also not used to being President of the United States before—the enormity of his position hit him. A couple weeks ago, he was nearly pissing his pants in a hotel room off the turnpike. Now he was sitting in the most powerful office in the world.

He wielded powers that were unprecedented, but how much of that power was truly in his hands and who would obey his orders? Much of the country had been placed in a state of emergency and martial law. The military surrounded New Jersey, and the PCRC Security Forces were running things inside the state.

Who were these PCRC men and women now in charge of security—both his own and the state's? Soon, these contractors might be controlling the security of the nation. They presented themselves as if they were a military organization, but they weren't. They were mercenaries, hired guns. Would they be loyal to him or to the PCRC organization that paid their salary? To Maxwell Gold alone?

The military took a solemn oath to support and defend the Constitution of the United States and to obey the orders of the President of the United States.

Law enforcement took an oath to serve and protect the public.

PCRC contractors took a piss test.

Maxwell walked into Patrick's office and closed the door behind him, nearly physically pushing the trailing Mr. Spencer. The man was suffering nothing but indignities today.

"Mr. President," Maxwell began in a placating tone. "You asked to see me?"

Patrick clasped his hands together. "I asked that you continue your meeting in here. Who were you meeting with?"

"The meeting had just wrapped up. It was not anything to concern yourself with."

"Who was it with?" Patrick snapped.

Maxwell raised his eyebrow like a professor whose pupil was being insolent. "It was with the head of transportation for the state." Maxwell enunciated each syllable with a little pop. He acted calm, yet irritated. "We were discussing the secure transport of freight in and out of the state as soon as the borders are reopened. My next meeting is with the head of sanitation. The department is concerned about waste management and ensuring our containment teams are not mixing of biohazard materials with standard trash. Would you like to join in on that meeting?"

Patrick knew he was being talked down to. He had not slept more than two hours at a time over the past two weeks and was in no mood for condescension. His nights were spent obsessively reading the comments under every news story featuring his name. The hatred of these trolls burned through their keyboards and came at him like thousands of tiny daggers.

"I saw men in uniforms. Generals," Patrick said. "Were they here to talk about trash transport also?"

"No, that was not a general, it was an admiral from the Navy that was here to brief us on those abandoned ships floating off the coast. The unfortunate sailors who were infected have been consolidated to a single vessel that is housing them in quarantine until a cure is found. The other two ships are being decontaminated and will be moved into deeper water, replaced by Coast Guard craft that will now take over the shore protection."

Maxwell recounted his allegedly dull meetings. "A representative from the Army was here yesterday to discuss repurposing some equipment that is returning from Afghanistan. With the war winding down, they are looking to sell off some of their extra assets, armored vehicles, deployable buildings, et cetera. They are offering PCRC some deals if we purchase in larger quantities. After all, I still have a business to run, and I have been buying the military's hand-me-downs for years—long before I served you as president, and even before I served you your first slice of cake at your eighth grade graduation party. Is this of concern to you?"

Patrick did not appreciate having things explained to him like he was still in eighth grade. He rose from his chair and stood behind his desk. "I'm sorry Max. I think I'm just tired. Getting grumpy. I apologize for interrupting you."

Maxwell faked a smile. "Of course, and you are never interrupting me. I am here to serve you and your administration. I apologize for holding my business meetings here. It is not professional; this is the Oval Office for now, and I should treat it as such," Maxwell said, forcing humility that felt like hot ash in his mouth.

Both stood there, looking at each other, waiting to see if either would offer one last fake apology.

Maxwell turned and opened the office door and walked out, brushing past Spencer, whose ear was still warm from having it pressed up against the door.

Patrick walked towards the door. Spencer, still outside, began to ask if he should continue his briefings, but did not get to finish his sentence as Patrick slowly closed the door in his face.

26

SUNDOWN

BMW flew his helicopter to the location of the final transponder ping. It was the last known location of the stolen truck containing MEAT. 7322 and Daniel sat behind the pilot in the passenger section along with 9104. She'd been chosen to replace 0303, who was still suffering from the indignities thrust upon him.

As dusk settled, Daniel looked down at the empty streets.

"Where the hell is everyone?" Daniel said to no one in particular.

7322 said, "Sundown curfew. New rules until this situation is resolved."

Daniel scoffed. "Since when the hell does anyone in Jersey obey the rules? I don't even see any of your patrols out there. What's stopping them from going out if they want to?"

"We are keeping the heavy security presence consolidated to the urban zones," 7322 explained. "Out here, in middle-class land, heavy handed enforcement is not really needed. You see the people in these upper middle class areas, they own their own homes, drive two cars, and have the obligatory two point five kids, usually in private schools. They don't require the forced compliance that other areas do. The reason most of these people have those nice houses and cars and privately educated kids is, basically, because they follow the rules. Societies have rules, and by most counts, those that follow the rules succeed."

"People are not going to take this martial law crap too much longer," Daniel warned. "Sooner or later, if this drags on, people will get pissed."

7322 took on a dismissive tone. "Sure they will. I am sure we will receive some harshly worded emails or be the subject of some terse tweets. I think we will be able to weather that storm. Ultimately, most people will fall in line. They are sacrificing a little bit of their personal freedoms for a greater feeling of security. Happens all the time. When changes in routine are announced, and the public is told to comply for their own safety, people usually don't push back that hard. They just adapt. If I told you before September 2001 that we would have domestic surveillance, strip searches before boarding a commercial flight, bomb scanners at football games, all that, you would have laughed in my face. Well, it's policy now. People don't like punishment, but they understand policy. These new rules are not punishment, they're just policy."

Daniel thought for a moment. Then shook his head. "That's bullshit. No one is entitled to get on a plane, just like you're not entitled to drive a car. People are willing to get a driver's license before they drive, and get a gun permit before they buy a gun. Now, you're restricting when people can and can't leave their own homes." Daniel pulled at the collar of his new black tactical outfit and pointed to the 8150 identifier. "People are entitled to wear what they want to wear, and to have their own name and identity, not numbers."

"Okay," 7322 continued. "I can use a more apt analogy. You and your brothers all went to Catholic high school, correct? And had to wear the school uniform every day?"

"Yeah, we started in public school, but my brother and I were kicked out in fourth grade."

7322 nodded. "I went to a private school as well. It was not a religious school, but a private institution where we also wore uniforms."

"I bet you looked *adorable,*" Daniel said.

7322 ignored the crack and carried on. "While you were in Catholic school, you had dress down days where you could wear whatever you wanted. I bet you looked forward to those days, excited to wear the same type of clothes you did when you were in public school before you were busted for stealing and selling your teachers' weed."

Daniel thought back to a much happier time in his life. "Yeah, that's true. Wait, how the fuck do you know so much about me?"

"I have been working for Max for a long time," 7322 replied.

Daniel had no idea where this analogy was going. "So what's your point?"

7322 smiled. "So when you were in public school, you used to wear whatever you wanted, every day. But then, when the situation changed, you followed the new rules and policies and wore a school uniform every day. You didn't like it, but you adjusted. Then, later on, as a reward for good behavior or a school success, the kids were given a little bit of their freedom back. Something they used to take for granted, wearing jeans and a t-shirt to school. But now you and the rest of the kids are jumping for joy to get a single day of that self-determination back. I bet you even thanked the principal for granting it and allowing you to wear jeans. Imagine that, being thankful for a single day of personal freedom, something that you used to have every day and took for granted."

Daniel had never looked at it that way.

7322 ended the lesson. "When you went to your new Catholic school, they did not take the freedom away from you as 'punishment.' I bet if they had allowed it to seem like a punishment, you would have rebelled, tore up the uniform, wore jeans every day till the principle cracked or kicked you out. But since it was just the new *policy* you had to live by under the new circumstances, you accepted it.

"Later, when they gave you little bits of that freedom back as a reward, you were grateful for the gift. Funny how that works, huh? What is important is that the public sees these new restrictions and rules as policy under a changed circumstance. It's not punishment, it's just policy."

27
DRIVE-THROUGH

BMW set the chopper down in the parking lot of a fast food restaurant called Happy Burger. The lot was an open area closest to where the last truck transponder ping had been recorded. This was in a residential area of central Jersey. The burger place appeared open for business, with all lights on, but they could see through the windows that the place was empty. Across the street stood a local steakhouse that also appeared open and had many cars in the parking lot. Curfew approached fast, so diners should be finishing up and heading home.

The crew took a visual survey of the area from inside the copter, but saw no sign of people, alive or...whatever. BMW shut his machine down and the blades slowed and grew still.

They saw no immediate sign of the missing truck.

"Hold up, I have to use the restroom," 9104 announced and began walking towards the entrance of the Happy Burger.

"Whoa, ma'am, we need to be careful," BMW warned.

"What are you afraid of?" 9104 said as she opened the glass door to the fast food joint and yelled in "Hey! Any zombies in here? Wooo hooo, zombies, come out come out wherever you are."

7322 shook his head. He knew 9104 before their current positions within PCRC. She had always been a ball buster. Probably a defense mechanism from being an attractive woman who wanted to show she could hang with the guys. She had worked for the police department as a hostage negotiator, and thus was trained to stay calm in very tense situations. She also had the ability to calm others. She had left the force and joined PCRC after a call out went exceptionally bad. A successful negotiation should end with no use of force and both victims and perp unharmed.

9104's final call out ended with everyone dead, including some kids.

When PCRC announced the formation of the new security contractor force, she was one of the first to join.

"This area has had no recent reports of infected, so we should be okay," 9104 assured her counterparts.

Nothing responded to her taunts. She entered and the others followed.

The place was indeed empty, yet all the lights were on, the doors unlocked, and the grills seemed to have shut down automatically as burned pucks that were once cooking burgers lay cold and black on the grill. The dining area was messy, but no more so than a typical fast food joint after a busy night.

9104 made a beeline towards the ladies' room. 7322 sat down at one of the window booths and kept an eye out for movement. Daniel and BMW made their way behind the counter to see if anything edible was readily available.

"See if the soda machine still works, I need a drink," Daniel suggested.

BMW walked towards the soda fountain, and it was there that he first saw the blood splatter around the small cove where workers would stand to deliver drive-through orders. The retractable window there was cracked and hanging off its hinges. The floor was covered with cups, lids, straws, condiment packets, and blood.

"Shit, whatever happened here happened at the drive-through," BMW said.

Daniel grumbled. "Maybe they messed up the wrong guy's order. Not getting the right happy meal toy can do that to you."

"I hate the drive-through, they always screw it up."

Their joking was a cover for nervousness. Both men had encountered Skells several times already and knew how fast things can go bad.

7322 stood up, turning his head so he could look at both them while keeping an eye out the window. A monitor displayed static above the cracked window. He said, "That must be the security camera that records drivers as they approach for the order and captures images of assholes who start trouble."

Daniel reached up and hit the rewind button.

The digital recording jumped back to the beginning of the session. A timestamp told them it was yesterday. Daniel reached up again and hit fast forward. It sped through a typical day. People zooming through to grab their cheap grub.

Then two Happy Burger employees appeared obviously agitated on the screen.

Daniel hit play. The action slowed to normal speed. While there was no sound, it showed an SUV rolling up to the drive through at high speed and sideswiping the building. The car backed up, scraped along the wall of the building, then came to a stop. When the driver's side window was perfectly aligned with the take out window, the driver, a woman, was acting erratically. Rocking violently back and forth in her seat as if throwing a tantrum. The two workers seemed to be trying to talk with her through the window, perhaps to calm her down or identify why she was so manic.

The woman then slammed her fist into her own stomach. Over and over. Like she was trying to beat something out of herself. The girl behind the window reached out to try and stop her, but it was a fatal mistake.

The woman turned her rage away from her own stomach and grabbed the burger girl. She caught hold of the girl's uniform and hair and violently pulled her partially out of the order window.

Two coworkers ran to the girl's aid, but by now the woman was biting large chunks of the flailing burger girl's face. Parts of her cheek came away in ragged, bloody heaps. A man in a white, short sleeved dress shirt ran into the picture, possibly the manager, and joined in on the attempt to pull the girl back in. Another coworker could be seen on a cell phone, pacing, perhaps calling 911.

A second car rammed into the vehicle's rear, pushing the SUV forward. The mad woman driver had not let go of the burger girl. Her body got pulled out the window.

One of the counter girls covered her face and ran out of view. The manager leaned out the window, looking for where the SUV had gone, not realizing the car behind was populated by a driver attempting to escape his ravenous two children in the back seat. A fiendish back-seat monster-child reached his body through the car window and grabbed the manager, yanking his arm forward and biting it, removing a mouthful of hairy forearm flesh.

The horrified fast food manager pulled his wounded arm back and ran from the camera's field of view. The father of the two monster boys must have managed to get his foot back on the accelerator—his car sped out of frame just as one of the children was using its teeth to peel back the man's scalp like the skin of a grapefruit. Rivulets of blood cascaded down his face.

The camera kept recording the drive-through area, but it only showed shadows of the pandemonium in the restaurant until the system ran out of digital storage space and stopped.

The time stamp told them that this horrific scene had been recorded earlier today. What 7322 wondered was why he saw no reports from this area of Skell activity. He thought that someone would have wandered in and seen the scene and reported it by now. A PCRC clean up team should have been dispatched immediately, and within a couple hours, depending on the severity of the carnage, would have made the location of the attack look as if nothing had ever happened.

Someone had really dropped the ball here.

Or, perhaps, there was no one left to report what happened.

The ladies' room door slammed against the wall. 9104 burst out, her hands around the neck of a ragged, bloody man. The two of them spun together and bounced off the walls like a pinball.

28
GUTLESS

The three men pulled their guns

9104 held the bloody man with a stiff arm as he extended his head and neck forward, snapping his jaw at her. "Kill him!" she cried. She gave one last spin and threw herself backwards away from the attacker.

Daniel instinctively shot the man in the head. He scored a hit between the eyes. A bucket load of brain matter blasted out the back of its skull, but the man's rage was only briefly halted. The infected straightened himself into a standing position and resumed his march towards Daniel.

Daniel got off two more rounds, but the Skell was quick and Daniel lost his footing, falling backwards on the greasy restaurant floor. BMW kicked the attacker hard in the side and the man flew off Daniel and rolled across the floor.

The attacker scrambled, his teeth biting the air in anticipation, and rushed again for Daniel.

Daniel pulled the tactical knife from his hip and stabbed upwards into the attacker's stomach. He dragged the blade sideways, slicing open the Skell's abdomen, allowing the stomach to squish down. The attacker became confused and ceased his attack. Daniel pushed the gore-soaked man off and stood, backing away from the scene. The Skell slowly rose, a good part of its guts hanging out of the gaping wound. The stomach sloshed forward and fell out of the incision. The large organ, suspended by the esophagus, swung back and forth like a pendulum in front of the Skell's legs.

The Skell took a slow single step forward, then another. He was alive, but winding down, as if he were falling asleep.

It was then that Daniel and BMW noticed the strange, grotesque formation of the stomach. Even though they had never seen the entire organ up close, Daniel had seen enough combat wounds to know that the human stomach should not look like what he was seeing.

The stomach had become a near perfect brain. Pale pink. Covered in folds.

BMW pointed at it. "What the fuck is that?!"

Daniel knew that you needed to shoot them in the stomach to put them down, but he didn't know why—until now.

Daniel gawked. "Is that their brain? Their fucking brain?"

7322 drew a long knife from its sheath on his side, inserted it where Daniel's original bullet had entered its skull, and with a flipping motion, lopped off the top of the man's head just above the bridge of its nose. The creature swung its arm as if swatting away a fly, but it kept plodding in the direction of Daniel.

Daniel stood on the tips of his toes and BMW stepped up for a closer look. They could see that within the cavity of his skull, there was nothing but a small pile of black goo sloshing around.

7322 motioned with his hand. "Welcome to the future. Now you see what we're up against." He used the same knife to slice the intestine keeping the stomach-brain attached to the body, allowing it to fall to the floor with a wet thud.

The Skell it had occupied immediately went limp and crumpled to the floor, no longer a danger.

Daniel sputtered. "Wait. So...so...wait."

BMW managed a "What the fuck!"

Daniel stammered, trying to form his question. "S-s-so...wait..."

7322 said, "I don't pretend to understand the science behind this, but yes, their stomach is their brain. It takes some time after infection to fully form. This gentleman must have been infected for at least forty-eight hours to have become so advanced. He has had some time to undergo the transformation."

Daniel blinked. "So...wait."

"*Okay,* I will let your minds digest what you just saw," said 7322 in a rare attempt at humor. "I need to call this in. Stay here and try not to attract any more Skells."

7322 walked outside to the chopper. Daniel and BMW stood in stunned silence staring at the spectacle in front of them. BMW stepped forward, extended his leg, and poked at the stomach brain with his shoe.

Daniel threw up a hand. "Dude, knock that shit off. Thing might still be alive."

7322 returned with a case, placed it on a table, and unbuckled the latches. "If your minds are functioning again, I can tell you what I know. These things are transforming in more ways than meets the eye. We all know that they consume and digest human flesh. The virus causes accelerated body fat absorption, which is why they are thin. They are absorbing their own flesh. As their brain dissolves, their stomach compensates by forming its own brain."

He removed the Shit Storm weapon from the case. "It's not a real brain. It can't really think, it can't reason, no higher functions that would allow the infected to communicate."

BMW said, "So these things function on impulse?"

"Exactly, they only know what they need to survive, which is human flesh." He pointed to BMW and Daniel. "Which is *you*."

Daniel said, "Sounds like some strippers I used to know."

7322 ignored Daniel's comment. "So everything else is gone, just base instincts. Killing, eating, reproducing."

"You mean these things are screwing?"

7322 looked at Daniel and rolled his eyes. "Disgusting, and no, they are not screwing. They reproduce via transmission of the virus. Bites. Those that do manage to escape being eaten completely will eventually turn. It could take minutes to hours, depending on the bite, the size of the victim. A child can turn almost immediately. A morbidly obese adult could take most of a day."

"So the only way to kill these things is by gutting them?"

"No, they are human, they can die from almost anything that would also kill us. It is just that their internal organs are adapting, evolving. They need oxygen, but they can absorb it through their skin. They don't need a mouth and windpipe like we do. We have seen some without heads that can still function."

7322 handed the Shit Storm device to BMW. "Here you go, quick draw, but promise me, no more purposefully aiming it at uninfected." He then focused on Daniel, BMW and 9104, whom until that moment had not been briefed on the full effects of the infection. "Now you know what we are dealing with, but our task right now is not to kill these people, nor round them up. Our sole job is to find that truck, and hopefully the contents, and then head back south to Cape May. That is *it*. Please, no deviations."

The four of them walked back out into the parking lot. 9104 jumped on a dumpster at the rear of the building and then pulled herself up onto the roof of the Happy Burger. She surveyed the area and saw no movement, but she spotted the truck parked in an empty lot behind the steak house. She pointed it out to her cohorts and climbed back down.

They quietly marched towards the restaurant. It was a nice place, nestled on an otherwise residential side of the street. It appeared family owned, not a chain. Perfect place to sell off stolen steaks in a hurry. This must have been the hijackers' last stop.

A large fence separated them from the steak house parking lot, so they decided to maneuver around the block rather than risk the noise that would come with cutting or climbing the chain link fence.

As the three walked around the block, they saw house after house with lights on, but no movement.

"Man, something just ain't right here," BMW said in a hushed tone to Daniel. "All these houses have their front doors open. People don't leave their front door open."

Daniel kept his voice down too. "Neither of us grew up in a town like this. You know, idyllic and shit. Maybe people here always leave doors open and cars running." He knew this was ridiculous, but he just wanted to finish the job and get gone.

"Bullshit," BMW countered. "There ain't no place *that* idyllic. People don't leave their houses wide open when they're not around."

"Agreed," 9104 chimed in from behind the two men. Neither Daniel nor BMW realized she was listening in. "What?" she said, giving them a shrug. "You think I can't hear you? I know you fly a helicopter, but did you learn to whisper in one?"

BMW noticed her appeal. "Well, maybe if we survive this, I will take you up for a spin and you can teach me how to better modulate my speech volume."

It was then that both Daniel and BMW realized 7322 was staring daggers at them—they were moving in on his territory.

Daniel continued the banter. "Hey Niner," he said to 9104. "It's just that BMW isn't used to walking through a nice neighborhood like this at dusk and not seeing all the doors and windows being quick slammed shut and locked. You know, racial profiling and what not. All he needs is a hoodie."

"Go to hell, Sullivan," BMW said through a laugh. "They see you coming down the sidewalk, they think a shaved gorilla escaped the zoo."

"How about we stow the chit chat," 7322 hissed.

They arrived at the truck and Daniel jumped up to the driver's side door of the cab. It was empty, but the door was unlocked and the keys were sitting right on the passenger seat. An invitation for a thief to come take it away.

"Well, this is going to be a lot easier than I thought," Daniel said with relief. "Get in. I'll drive you guys back to the bird and meet you back at—"

He was interrupted by a horrified shriek from 9104.

29
#ZOMBIEDIET

From the Diet Underground blog:

Hello and goodbye, Diet Underground readers. This is Donut_destroyer66, and this is my final blog post.

I am going to share a weight loss secret with you, and then I am logging off, and deleting my account, and forgetting it ever existed. In fact, I am going to forget the old, fat me ever existed as well.

The reason I will be vanishing from our cyber fat forum is because what I am going to share is controversial. If it worked for me, it can work for you. But I don't want to hear from any of you who screw up and get hurt or killed. You can take my advice at your own risk. Any haters out there or anyone looking to file a lawsuit, please stop reading right now. If you are still reading, I am about to give you the magic secret to massive weight loss.

Last week I was over 500 pounds, and today, I look like a flagpole. How?

Did I go on the Oprah diet? What a joke. Unless the Oprah diet means eating Oprah's weight in ice cream, I would never have lasted a day on it. Did I have surgery? Nope. Exercise? Give me a fucking break.

So how did I do it? All I can tell you is that I was in a McDonalds enjoying my third quarter pounder with cheese when this emaciated, bloody, freak staggered into the place. It took a minute, but everyone realized it was one of those infected Skell people. The customers went crazy and started running for the doors. I was about to do the same, but realized I was stuck in my chair. No, not frozen with fear, but actually stuck between the bolted to the ground chair and table.

By the time I extracted myself, it was just the two of us, the zombie and I. The thing came at me and I knew I could not outrun it. So what did I do? I sumo'd the goddamn thing. I ran directly at it while it was coming directly at me. The thing hit my stomach and bounced backwards and landed on its back. It was scrambling up, so I threw myself on top of it to hold it down, but the thing was so emaciated, I crushed it and its insides popped out underneath me like a squished grape. I stood back up, puked, and then I hauled my fat ass out of there.

I don't know what the rules are now. Can you just kill zombies when you see them? Do you have to wait for those black pajama wearing storm trooper guys to show up to haul them away? Am I going to get sued for killing it in some sort of zombie court?

I did not want to find out, so I just took off.

I got home, threw my clothes away, and took a shower. It was then that I noticed a small amount of blood coming from the fold underneath my right chest area. I felt underneath and found two Skell teeth stuck in my skin. I did not even realize I had been bitten.

I was scared that if I went to the hospital, they would report me, and then I would be taken to one of those freaky FEMA camps they are setting up. So I kept my pie hole shut and told no one.

That night, my stomach was going nuts. I was sweating, puking, farting. I rushed to the bathroom with the Hershey squirts like no one's business. I punished my toilet. It was as if I was melting through my pores and out my anus.

Sometime during the night, I finally passed out and had the most insane dreams ever. It was like someone or something was conscious inside of me and trying to control me. Like my own mind was fighting with a foreign mind trying to invade me.

It was an epic battle, but when I finally came to—nearly 30 hours later—I raised my head off the pillow, looked down, and saw something I had not seen for years: my feet.

I dragged myself over to the bathroom and looked in the mirror. The sight of the stranger before me made me fall backwards into my bathtub. I looked around for the intruding bastard and realized I was alone. The stranger in the reflection was me. I am now about 120 pounds! I am not kidding you. I dropped a few hundred like a snake shedding its skin.

It must have been the bite. I got bit, but not enough to turn me full zombie. Just enough for me to drop down to a thirty-inch waist.

So do what you want out there, my fellow fatties, my porcine partners, my chubby chums. I am not telling you to go out and get bit, and I don't know if I am going to keep losing weight, or maybe turn into one of those Skells, but for now, I am going out and getting laid!

Goodbye from the former Donut_destroyer66. #zombiediet

30
VINNI, VIDI, VICI

TO: All Post Conflict Restoration Corp Employees
FROM: PCRC Marketing & Communications Department
Memorandum to all PCRC Contractors.
RE: Rules of Infection Engagement
This is a directive for all PCRC contractors involved in citizen-facing roles.

- PCRC Containment Teams
- PCRC Security Teams
- PCRC Collection Teams

As you are aware, PCRC is the exclusive contract holder for managing the current security situation. While we do not fully understand the impact of the virus and how it affects individual victims, we are aware of four distinct types of infected individuals, to be referred to as Patients.

In security, containment, and collection roles, you may encounter anyone one of the four following classifications of patients.

1. Virus Infected Individuals (VII's). Upon initial infection, depending on the size of the individual, and severity of the transmission, the individual may be infected, highly contagious, but showing no signs of contagion or symptoms. These individuals are to be immediately quarantined in established camps (Q Camps). See Civilian Infection Protocol 2.1 for additional information.

2. Virus Infected Deceased (VIDs). These are unfortunate individuals who have succumbed to the virus or injuries incurred during the infection (usually through a violent encounter with another infected individual) or injuries incurred post infection (usually through a violent encounter with an uninfected individual). VIDs are to be treated as extremely dangerous biohazardous materials. Please review the documentation provided on specimen handling and bio surveillance.

3. Virus Infected Necrotic (VINs). VINs have fully succumbed to the infection and are to be collected and transferred to quarantine camps for housing until a cure can be identified. VINs, which have been referred to in the public as Skells, may

exhibit distended stomachs and are most easily neutralized via broadcasting the hum. They will congregate around PCRC sound and security systems, which have been deployed around the state. While they may appear docile, they are to be treated with extreme caution. They can become extremely violent and there is a 100% chance of transmission of the virus though their bites.

4. Virus Infected Non-Necrotic Individuals (VINNIs). These are to be treated with utmost care. VINNIs are subjects who have managed to survive the wasting effects of the virus. The virus appears to either pause, or burn itself out completely within these individuals. There is initial evidence that these may have been individuals who were suffering from morbid obesity prior to infection. VINNIs are lean, muscular, and do not exhibit the full, distended stomachs that are found on VINs. They retain their full mental and emotional abilities and would appear to be virus-free. But please note, these individuals are extremely dangerous, can still transmit the virus, and are not biologically the same as they were prior to infection. To repeat, while they appear to be the same, they are *no longer* as they once were. They are biologically altered.

VINNIs must be detained at all cost and reports or encounters with VINNIs must be immediately reported to your PCRC Contract Supervisor. VINNIs are to be treated with care and should be considered extremely dangerous.

If a VINNI is acquired, they are to be transferred directly to the nearest Q Camp.

Thank you for your absolute compliance with these directives. Any deviation can result in loss of contractor status and immediate termination.

Nick Letterman

VP, Marketing

31

"THAT WHOLE BRAIN-MELTING, FLESH-EATING THING"

9014 had opened the bay doors at the rear of the truck and what she encountered was so horrific the always calm, tough as nails, crisis negotiator let out an involuntary scream as if she were a ten-year-old girl.

The truck was filled from floor to ceiling with bodies. Mangled, decapitated, and torn limb from limb. They appeared to have been drawn and quartered. A flood of blood and guts spilled out of the back as the doors opened, splashing to the ground in a waterfall of gore. There were hundreds of them. They all appeared to be Skells, but with the remains in such a state, ripped apart or split in half, it was impossible to tell.

Sudden blinding illumination lit up the truck as two large military style Humvees roared up and stopped near them.

The PCRC gang shielded their eyes and could see only the silhouettes of soldiers as they exited from the vehicles and approached holding assault rifles.

One of them barked an order: "Drop your weapons now!"

7322 reached for his pistol.

"Don't try it asshole!" one of the other men yelled, pointing his gun at 7322's head.

"You, out of the cab!" they shouted to Daniel.

He complied and tossed his gun to the ground, as did 7322 and 9104. Each raised their hands.

One by one, the headlights and floodlights were turned off.

Daniel could see a man exit the first car along with two additional heavily armed troops. The two guards stayed back at the vehicle, pointing their weapons at Daniel and his crew, while the one man walked over to the second and then a third vehicle, reaching into the driver's side window and flicking off the lights of each.

This new man was not in uniform. As the last of the blinding headlights went dark, Daniel saw that the other men with him were not soldiers either, but private security forces, hired muscle, just as 7322 and 9104 were—just as Daniel and BMW now were as well.

The non-uniformed man approached them.

He was older, dressed casual in slacks, shirt and suit jacket. He looked familiar. "I figured Gold would send one of the mutant brothers. Always out fetching sticks, huh Sullivan?"

Daniel knew this guy, but again, he could not place it.

"Where's my son, Sullivan?" The man asked tersely.

Pinskey! Daniel thought to himself. It was Pinskey from that escort mission in Pakistan that went to hell. He was in the building when a truck bomb took it down. They assumed he was dead.

This is why that kid, Eric Pinskey, was so important to Maxwell Gold.

Daniel began putting the pieces together. "He's fine, I took him out of New Jersey. I did not know you were even alive."

"I am." Pinskey jutted his chin out. "Obviously."

"Look, if this is just about your kid, I had no idea. Max told me he was important and to protect him. I did." Daniel 's eyebrows lifted on his face. "I got him out of the state, he is safe and fine." He tried to appear reassuring.

"I am glad to hear that, Mr. Sullivan. I thought this was going to be a difficult transaction, so I attempted to acquire Mr. Gold's son for some leverage. As we know, that did not work out so well for either of us," Pinskey said with an ominous tone.

Daniel had been briefed about what went down at Ivan's backup compound at the old school. Two men had tricked their way in, convincing Daniel's brother Gerald that they were some of Ivan's followers and that they were supposed to meet him at that location. Once in, they managed to capture Ivan. Ivan's wife Marifi had gotten hold of one of the abductors and proceeded to brutally torture him until they released Ivan. There was some sort of shootout and in the aftermath, several were killed, including the two men Pinskey had sent and Gerald Sullivan.

"So...this is all about that kid?" Daniel asked angrily. "My brother is dead because I protected your kid?"

"It's not just about the kid," 7322 said, letting on he knew who Pinskey was as well.

"Correct, Mr. Two," Pinskey said with a small mocking bow to 7322. "May I call you by your surname, Two? Or do I call you by the informal Seven? Proper etiquette is difficult to figure out in Gold's new world of numbers instead of names. He should just tattoo bar codes on your forehead. But I guess tattooing numbers on one's body is a touchy subject for his kind."

7322 looked down at the number on his uniform.

"Surely you all realized PCRC had competitors," Pinskey said. "We are very interested in this MEAT product your employer developed. The Modified Embryonic Animal Tissue. While obviously its initial launch was less than a success," he waved his hand toward the truckload of mutilated Skells, "we feel that it has great potential. If we could just tweak the formula, we know that this product would be of great benefit. A meat replacement system that is not only delicious, but addicting. It's like chocolate, cigarettes, and heroin, all mixed up in one tasty filet. We always appreciate addicted consumers, just not as ravenous as your current clientele." An evil smile took over his face.

Pinskey had been involved with the MEAT research operation as a key supplier for PCRC, providing human stem cells for what the PCRC had said was scientific experimentation. He put all the pieces together when he found out about the plan for MEAT. Realizing that the only way he was going to fully capitalize on this knowledge was to go off on his own, he had coordinated the fake attack in Pakistan himself. The plan was to have Maxwell Gold believe he died, and he needed to leave at least one Sullivan brother alive to report his demise.

"Your employer invented the ultimate American consumable. Eat all you want and skip the gym membership. Easy answers to complex problems. Isn't that what he always offered? Need to get out of a jam, call Maxwell Gold. Not getting the resources you want from of a foreign country, call Maxwell to send in his dogs to start a civil war. Uh oh, got a dead guy on the floor in the White House, he just shot himself in the Lincoln bedroom. Call Maxwell, he will make it look like a suicide that took place in the park miles away. Easy answers."

7322 spoke up: "Do you really think this can be controlled, that the cause of this nightmare won't happen again and again if you keep down this path?"

Pinskey maintained his wretched grin. "Stick to doing what you're told and let us figure things out. This is a simple matter of formula. Maxwell's team almost got it right, but they launched too early. A little more research and development time and he would have been given the Nobel Prize. We just need to find the right formula to make it so once weight loss begins, it actually ceases before they become walking skeletons. Oh, and then of course, there was that whole brain melting, flesh-eating thing. But what do they say? If at first you don't succeed..."

32
PAY THE SOUL TOLL

Colonel Tindall was in final preparations to move his soldiers out of the cul-de-sac under cover of darkness. Smoothie came downstairs from a nap and found the soldiers packing their gear. He walked into the dining room to find Colonel Tindall still holding his bible. He was wrestling internally whether to put it back in his pocket or leave it behind.

Tindall decided against taking the book and tossed it onto the table.

"I never understood one thing about church," Smoothie commented on the conversation that no one was having. "Well, I guess there are lots of things I don't understand about church. I probably could save time and just list for you the few things I *do* understand. I mean, you go to church, and you see these people all dressed up and sitting there in the pews on Sunday like that is the only time God sees them. I know a lot of the people that went to my church, and some were real sinners. Like 'winning the championship of sinning' sinners."

"You can forget all that dogma you heard in church about the end of days," Tindall said. "This current situation has nothing biblical or godly about it. This apocalypse is manmade."

Smoothie felt like a debate. "Jesus was a man. If Jesus made something happen, then it would be manmade, correct?"

"Yes, but this was a created in a lab. No one turned water into wine here—this was chemistry," Tindall countered.

"How do you know Jesus didn't turn water into wine through chemistry? Maybe he figured out some formula and it's been lost to the ages. Or, perhaps, it was just a magic trick, but he told everyone it was a miracle to appear important?"

Tindall furrowed his brow. Frustration bloomed inside him. "Jesus was important."

"Yep," Smoothie agreed. "Jesus raised the dead and he himself rose from the dead, so perhaps this is all his doing."

"This ain't that!" Tindall snapped.

"How do you know?"

Tindall raised his chin in the air and rubbed his eyes. "Those super sinners you knew, the ones who still showed up to church every Sunday. They are not real Catholics, they are called 'lapsed Catholics,' people who think you can act the fool all week and then every Sunday wipe their soul clean like they do their browser history."

Smoothie shifted his weight from one foot to the other. He knew his browser history couldn't be cleaned with bleach. "Yeah, true, but isn't that the bargain Catholics sign up for? Confess your sins, pay your penance, and be forgiven?"

Colonel Tindall leaned back in his chair. "I feel like New Jersey has perfected the art of sin. The governor of this state should set up confessional toll booths on the parkway so people can drive through, pay the soul-toll with their E-ZPass, and get their forgiveness receipt emailed to them each week." He looked upwards to the heavens. "Christ, why do I have to meet my judgment in Jersey?"

Jack Jones, otherwise known as Smoothie, smiled. He liked Tindall. Smoothie knew his family would be okay—his wife was tougher, smarter, and more resourceful than he ever was. Besides, it has been a long time since she wanted him around. Tindall was the type of man he had hoped he would become when he grew up. Issue was: Smoothie never grew up.

This might be my chance, he thought to himself. He never had a mentor, or someone to show him the way to become a man. A man that could take on the troubles of the world and have the respect and admiration of those around him. Maybe this was his chance to start over.

Right there, he made his decision. He would follow Colonel Tindall wherever it took him. He had found his mentor, and perhaps, he too could counsel this man, a man of decency, on how to navigate the depravity of the new world they would be facing.

It was his destiny.

33

TWEAKING THE FORMULA

Daniel's head was spinning with everything Pinskey had just told them.

"This is not something that can be managed. This needs to end," 7322 yelled to Pinskey. "This entire town has been wiped out, and you think that this can be prevented with some formula tweaking?"

"Exactly," Pinskey responded. "Hell, even New Coke didn't go over so well when first launched, but business is all about trial and error. Now, Mr. Sullivan, if you could please provide me the location of my son." He squinted at Daniel. "Then, after that, my friends and I would like to take a trip with you all back to Cape May."

"You won't get near the president," 7322 said.

"Oh, I couldn't care less about that puppet." Pinskey sneered. "I need to speak with the real man in charge.

And you three will assure me a personal audience with Mr. Gold. He and I have a lot of catching up to do."

9104 had managed crisis negotiations under the worst circumstances. She felt she could handle this: "Listen Pinskey, this is not some sort of corporate pissing contest. You don't need to push it any further. If you leave now and let us go, no one is going to get hurt. You're a businessman. You don't want blood on your hands."

Pinskey slowly strolled over to her.

7322 tensed.

"Really?' Pinskey said. And with that, he gave her an open-handed palm directly into her face, splitting her lip and knocking her to the ground.

7322 attempted to move forward, but the men with the guns stepped towards him.

Daniel did not react.

Pinskey reached down and grabbed 9104's face, his palm on her bloody mouth, and pulled her to her feet. He then looked at the blood on the palm of his right hand and wiped it together with his left.

"Hmm, looks like I now have blood on my hands." Pinskey said showing his blood stained palms to his hired troops.

His men chuckled.

He walked over to Daniel and wiped the blood off on Daniel's new uniform, making a show of it to demonstrate his control over the situation.

"Calm yourselves, this is not going to be for public consumption." Pinskey continued. "At least not yet.

First, we have an army to build. An army that does not need to be fed, but that feeds itself. These men you see behind me work for paychecks. The army I envision will see no need for money." He turned to one of his hired mercenaries. "You there, zip-tie their hands."

Pinskey's gunman took two steps forward and began gagging as if he had swallowed something foul. His wretches became more severe and he bent over and started vomiting profusely.

Everyone looked over at him, confused.

"He's infected!" 9104 shouted, pointing at the stricken man.

The puking man waved at them like he was trying to disagree, but he could not stop his projectile vomiting.

Pinskey and the others began to back away from him.

A second guard grabbed his stomach and bent over in pain. That man began vomiting while simultaneously letting out horrific blasts of flatulence.

"They're sick! They're all infected. Your men are infected!" 9104 yelled to Pinskey, who was obviously terrified and confused by what he was witnessing.

A third gunman let out a disgusting sound as if his entire bowels had emptied with the force of a freight train. He dropped to a squatting position and hobbled away behind one of the vehicles and started removing his pants.

Pinskey ran back to one of the Humvees, jumped in, and sped away. The remaining unaffected security also piled into their vehicles and fled, leaving behind the three stricken cohorts.

BMW jumped down from the roof of the truck onto the roof of the cab, then slid down the front to the ground, still holding the Shit Storm weapon.

9104 gathered up guns from the gastro-attacked mercenaries. Having the attractive woman relieve them of their weapons while they lay on the ground in a pile of their own filth was truly rubbing salt in the wound.

She walked over to the truck, still spitting out some blood, and threw the guns into the space behind the driver's seat.

Daniel reached his hand down and helped her up into the cab.

"You know, the Borg would have been a better analogy," she said to him.

"Huh?"

"Earlier today, when you and your friend put on the uniform. You said it was like *Body Snatchers*. That's a really old reference. The Borg is a *Star Trek* term for an enemy that assimilates everyone into their ranks."

"Yeah, well, I didn't watch that because I'm not a friggin nerd."

"Okay," she said, spitting more blood out the window. "You missed a good show."

"And besides," Daniel continued, "I don't see you as an enemy."

"That's good." She paused. "What do you see me as?"

Daniel cocked an eye. "A nerd."

They laughed.

34
SELLING THE APOCALYPSE

GRASS not only had a cybercrime unit, but also a marketing division. Since many of the members were millennials, they understood the power of proper messaging and communication online. Triston, Marcus, Joel, and Shoshanna had joined the movement together, leaving some of the most sought after public relations and advertising firms in the country.

Their specialty was in the realm of association and affiliation promotion, with a focus on launching political campaigns and new charitable organizations. If you were looking to create a labor movement like SEIU (Service Employees International Union), a national association like AARP, a reformation like Perestroika or a protest group like Occupy Wall Street or The Tea Party, you had probably worked with one of these four young individuals to create the message and launch the campaign. Together, they were the senior management of Autumn Marketing, LLC, based in Red Bank, NJ.

Triston, with a perfectly groomed, auburn beard that seemed too big for his slight frame, stood at the front of the table near the white board. Dry erase marker in his hand, he started off the meeting by asking Marcus if he could capture notes.

Marcus was the sole minority in the room. His afro large enough to demonstrate he was cool, but short enough to fit into the corporate culture. His work focused on creating specialty and social activist groups. Whenever a *message* needed a *group*, like Occupy Wall Street or The Moral Majority, Marcus was your guy.

Shoshanna was the lead on focus groups. All messaging needed to be tested, and she specialized in ensuring that the right combination of words and phrases were put together to nail home the point. Her job was to ensure that the proper color lipstick was put on the pig.

Joel was the lead on organization development. Movements didn't truly rise from the street. They took strategy and planning. You had to have the right people in the beginning. If you wanted to open a hot new restaurant, you needed shiny, skinny people in attendance so that the gray, boring-yet-wealthy people would be desperate for a reservation. Joel handled that. If you wanted to open an exclusive member's only club and have the richest and most influential people want to join, Joel was your guy. Also, if you were a guy looking for a guy, Joel was your guy.

Triston took a long sip of his Mocha Valencia half-caff, returned the cup to its coaster, and began the meeting. He raised the dry erase marker to the top of the white board and wrote:

It's the end of the world as we know it.

"Our mission for the GRASS movement is a bit unusual, but not too far from what we've done in the past," Triston began. "We are here to create the birth of an army. The development of an idea that will spark devotion within a large number of people. A message that will create a following, a following of everyday folks who will feel the need to get off their couches, out of their comfort zones, to leave their jobs, their families if necessary, and all their worldly possessions, and to coalesce around, or should I say, *behind,* a single man."

"Which man?" Joel asked.

Shoshanna sighed. "Don't tell me we're creating another pre-packaged boy band."

Triston shook his head. "The man is still TBD. The message is up to us, and no, this is not a boy band, nor a candidate, nor a lifestyle personality. We are creating the next cult, but with a leader who will wield more power than anyone in this country has ever seen."

Marcus raised his hand as if he had heard more than enough of the sales pitch. "Come on, Triston, is this another one of those fitness programs we had to market? Some sort of get thin retreat where we take a bunch of rich fatties to Brazil and make them follow some muscle guru again?"

"Ah, Marcus, this is much more intense. After this journey, there will be no returning to the life you once lived. But enough of the mystery." Triston reached under the table and brought out his very expensive leather briefcase. "How many of you have read post-apocalyptic fiction?"

The three seated staffers exchanged looks. It wasn't a genre of book that would have been on the Amazon wish list for anyone in the room.

Joel raised his hand sheepishly. "I read Stephen King's *The Stand* in high school."

"Excellent!" Triston exclaimed. "Who else?"

"Define post-apocalyptic," Joel said.

"Books or movies that take place after the end of everything. Nuclear war, plague, famine, pestilence, alien invasion. You know, real science fiction-type works," Triston explained.

Shoshanna spoke up. "My little sister has read all of those *Hunger Games* books." She herself had just finished the last in the series a week ago and was about to begin reading *The Giver.*

"Okay, I am going to give you guys a reading and viewing list tonight. I, too, have not seen nor read much in this genre, but I spent the day with several of the Blades of GRASS tech support guys—i.e., nerds—and I got a thorough education."

Joel rolled his eyes. "What's the purpose of this exercise?"

Triston smirked. "This has come from the top. From Ronan himself."

Raised eyebrows and impressed looks were exchanged around the table.

Triston nodded. "Ronan feels that we need more than a brute squad within the Blades of GRASS. We have the Cyber Army, now we need a real army. An army that will take our message forth and rule the scarred landscape of the post-apocalyptic world." Triston said this particular line of bullshit as dramatically as he could.

"Look, I don't want to be the naysayer here, but we are not exactly on the cusp of the apocalypse right now. I mean, Starbucks is still open," Joel said, motioning to Triston's cup of $9.00 coffee. "Of course, the wait at the shop downstairs has been really long, but that's because the head barista was eaten by a zombie on Monday and the new girl is still learning the order process."

"LaDonna was killed?" Shoshanna asked. "How awful, how did that happen?"

"What can I tell you, she was always a bleeding heart," Joel said with snark. "I guess you can hug a zombie, but just once."

Chuckles spread around the table.

"Joel, you are not taking the long view," Triston said. "Things are weird, but relatively calm *right now.* What about a year from now? Five years from now? Society will collapse, anarchy will reign. When that occurs, and we all agree that it is *when,* not *if,* we want to ensure the man leading the largest, toughest, most ruthless army of warriors is *our* man. You plan today to execute tomorrow. First in, first win."

Marcus cleared his throat. "Okay, so let me make sure I understand. In these books and movies you were talking about, there's always some sort of grassroots army of hundreds or thousands of followers that run the land. These apocalyptic armies come out of nowhere, and are led by some tough guy or psychopath who guides them across the urban blight, destroying everything in their path like a swarm of human locust and growing their ranks."

"*Exactly!*" Triston squealed, excitedly pointing at Marcus. "But we are not going to wait for someone to rise from the ashes. We need to carefully identify and choose this future leader."

"So we're looking to find a military leader?"

"Yes, but not necessarily the type you're thinking of. Military training would, of course, be beneficial, but they need to also be able to instill passion in their followers, a Genghis Kahn meets Jim Jones meets Lady Gaga type."

"Why does it have to be a guy?" Shoshanna asked to groans around the room.

"Okay, okay, sorry," she relented. "It's hard to turn the gender grievance card off."

Triston uncapped a different color dry erase marker with his mouth. "Let's get the creative juices going here. What would be some good names for this new army? Just shout it out, no bad ideas."

Shoshanna raised her hand. "I saw a movie on the plane over here, it involved a group of men who were lost in Alaska and were being hunted by a pack of wolves. That would be a pretty cool name. The Wolves."

Triston wrote it on the white board.

"The Wolves?" Marcus sneered. "It sounds like the name for a Midwestern high school football team. It's not intimidating. Why not the muskrats, or badgers?"

Triston clapped his hands. "Hey, like I said, no bad ideas. Let's keep it in the realm of sports teams. What would you name a football team if you owned one?"

"The Yankees?" Joel said.

"How about the Giants or the Raiders?" Marcus said. "Perhaps a synonym for Raiders?"

Shoshanna, a Georgetown graduate, chimed in. "How about the Redskins?

"Now, that name is just offensive."

"How about The Army of the New Savior," Joel said in a hushed tone.

Silence filled the room.

"Hmm. Savior? Interesting, a religious-themed name," Triston said, tapping the marker on his chin.

"We're going all-out religious here if we choose that type of name," Marcus said. "I guess religion is a kind of sport, but it isn't the one I was thinking of."

"Well, 'savior' has both religious and non-religions connotations."

"Why not then just call it the Army of Jesus," Marcus said with a shrug.

"Actually," Shoshanna butted in. "We focus-group tested 'Jesus' for a different campaign I worked on last year and the name Jesus came across as 'too pacifistic.' It's not aggressive or dominant sounding. So, I wouldn't recommend it. The term 'Christ' tested better, had a stronger connotation, more *oomph* to it. Tested very well." She paused. "But it was too religious. The term could be off-putting to many. We need that Goldilocks effect, not *too* hot, not to cold, just right."

Triston looked around the room. "Let me shake things up a bit, then. Why does it have to be an army? We're planning for a time of anarchy; an army connotes organization. What about a gang?"

"Nope." Shoshanna shook her head. "Tested it. 'Gang' has a weak, almost comical association. Our Gang, KC and the Sunshine Gang, Hole in the Wall Gang. Not threatening at all."

"Hey, Joel, don't you run in a clique called 'Hole in the Wall Gang?'" Marcus joked.

"Low blow," Joel shot back.

"No shit, that's the joke," Marcus replied, laughing heartily.

"Gloriously low!" Shoshanna added to the bawdy banter.

"Okay, okay, I think we're running into a dead end with names, so let's table this discussion and the jokes for now before I have a human resources issue on my hands."

Shoshanna said, "Aren't we getting ahead of ourselves here? This is like planning a wedding and we don't even have a groom yet. You said the leader of this new post-apocalyptic army needs to be a very specific type. Brutal, yet charismatic. Strong, yet intelligent.

Savior-like, but not overly religious. How do you suppose we're going to find such a chap? Match.com?"

Triston smiled and leaned forward on the table. "That's the best part. We already have two strong candidates we're currently tracking. They don't even know they're auditioning for the part of a lifetime. And, as if the fucking stars aligned to make it even more convenient, they are both already here in New Jersey, ground zero for the apocalypse. We just sit back and wait to see which of the two rises to the top." Triston grinned. "So, who's ready for lunch? Sushi anyone?"

35
VIXEN'S SCREAM

This is Dr. Zed with your Outbreak Update.

It is currently mating season the common fox. During this time, the female lets out a high, shrill call called the Vixen's Scream. Dr. Zed is familiar with this shrill vixen scream as he was once married.

Just kidding, folks.

This call is how the female fox finds a mate, and will repeat this cry multiple times in a row. This will occur in the evening or just before dawn. The Vixen's Scream is often mistaken for the scream of a woman or small child. Please note that if you hear this cry, you are asked not to go outside your home to investigate. Due to the current state of emergency, there are limited resources available for response, so please access the WALKR app on your data device and instead of taking a picture, click the emoji of the round yellow face shouting.

NEIL A. COHEN

This will notify PCRC Containment Teams that you have heard, but not seen, something. A team will arrive shortly to investigate.

Thank you and remember: Infection control is everyone's responsibility.

36
R.E.S.P.E.C.T

Marifi sat beside Ivan Gold while he drove their stolen Toyota, traveling only on back roads, weaving through roads littered with abandoned cars and sometimes mangled corpses. He was increasingly paranoid, requiring them to stay off the main roads and to switch cars every few miles. Ivan had a plan, he always had a plan, but he was not sharing it this time. Obviously, there was some reason he was taking them to Cape May. They had not said a word to each other for hours and had barely spoken at all since they left the burning boarding school two days earlier.

Ivan now knew that their courtship and marriage was a sham. That Marifi had been brought to the United States by Ivan's father for the sole purpose of marrying, and spying, on his son.

At least he did not know that, if given the order, she was to kill him as well. Perhaps he suspected. How such a father-son relationship could be so screwed up was beyond her.

By age 13, Marifi and her grandfather had settled in a small province of central Philippines called Pangasinan. It had been nearly a dozen years since her grandfather had fled the Manila Islamic Liberation Front after his daughter abandoned her own newborn daughter with him and vanished. He himself had been sold as a child to MILF, and although he had given them nearly fifty years of his life before fleeing, it was not enough. He was a deserter and would never feel safe. There was no statute of limitations on a lifetime of terror organization membership and he would forever have a price on his head with the sentence of death upon capture.

However, there in the small village of farmers, pigs, and goats, Marifi and her grandfather had settled into some sort of normalcy. Villagers did not ask too many questions as long as you kept to yourself and didn't cause trouble.

Due to her grandfather being raised in MILF since a child, he was basically illiterate, as his meager education consisted of the three R's: Rifles, Ransom, and Roadside Bombs. He only spoke an obscure southern Philippines dialect of Yakan, which was rarely used by anyone outside of extremely isolated Basilan Islands—a region dominated by terrorist organizations. He did not even speak the Philippine national dialect of Tagalog. In an effort not to raise questions about his background, he stayed mainly to himself while Marifi worked the fields to support them.

Her days were filled with odd jobs for pesos: clearing jungle brush, cleaning butchered hogs, and climbing trees to cut down green mangos and coconut. She enjoyed retrieving mangos and coconut the most, especially when she was able to work with her one friend, Gina.

Gina was a year older, but small in size due to a lifetime of malnutrition. The two would talk for hours, which made the menial labor in the heat go by faster than usual. It was a particularly humid day when Gina suggested they end their work early and walk the half mile through the jungle to a small clearing that housed some shops.

As they made their way, Marifi swung her Golok—a cross between a machete and a sword with a flat tip she used to retrieve mangos—to slice through the dense brush. They arrived in the clearing to see a Sari-Sari store, which was a family house with a metal shutter on one sidewall that could open to sell salty snacks, candy, and soda served in plastic bags. The vendor would pour the soda from a glass bottle into the plastic baggie and offer it up with a straw so that they could keep possession of the bottles for a refund.

Next door was a small shop selling flip-flop sandals, cheap plastic kitchen utensils, and straw hats. Across the street was a bar where dangerous men drank questionable liquor.

The two girls walked past three drunken men sitting outside the bar, and while no words were exchanged, the look in their eyes screamed foulness and obscenity.

They ignored the men and walked straight towards the soda. Gina ordered a bag.

"Do you have money?" The fat woman behind the counter asked with a rude, squinting look.

"Yes, we have money," Gina shot back, not intimidated by the woman's size or attitude. Gina was loud and confident, which Marifi admired.

The woman handed her a clear plastic baggie of soda with protruding straw and told her it was 50 pesos. Gina handed her the money. Marifi stepped up next and the woman handed her a soda bag, which Marifi consumed in nearly a single gulp.

"100 pesos," The woman snapped at Marifi.

"What?" Gina shouted. "Why is it more than mine?"

"There was more soda in hers," the lady replied.

"That is a lie!" Gina shot back.

Marifi reached into her pocket and pulled out 75 pesos. "This is all I have."

"You drank the soda, you owe me 100 pesos," The woman demanded.

"I don't have it." Marifi responded. She felt nervous. She didn't want this attention.

"Give me your Golok, then," said the lady, pointing at the large knife.

"No, this is my grandfather's. I need it for work." Marifi handed the woman her 75 pesos and hoped she would back off.

The woman yelled, waving her hands at them. "Get out of here you street cats!"

"We are leaving, and your soda was flat," Gina yelled back.

As the two turned to walk away, they realized three of the men from the bar had quietly positioned themselves directly behind them.

The fat woman slammed down the metal shutter of her shop.

A man with rotting teeth said, "Girls, where are your parents?"

The girls lowered their heads and began walking away, but two of the men positioned themselves to prevent escape. "Whoa, don't run away. We are friendly."

It was only then that the girls noticed how heavily armed the men were, each with a pistol in his waistband and rifles slung over their shoulders.

"Come with us, we have cold soda, you don't need to buy from that fat pig," another of the men suggested.

"Thank you, sir, we are fine, we need to get back to work," Gina said meekly.

"Please don't be rude, girls. You will be safe with us. Let's go," commanded the man with bad teeth.

Gina held her ground. "No thank you, sir, we must go."

"Girls, I will not ask again." He spoke without any of the fake kindness he initially used. He removed the gun from his waistband and made sure the girls could see it. "You are coming with us."

The three men herded the girls in front of them. One of the men grabbed the Golok from Marifi's hand and used it to point the girls in the direction they should begin walking, directly into the jungle, opposite the direction the girls came from and were familiar with.

As they headed into the jungle, Gina began to cry quietly. Neither knew what would become of them: raped, murdered, or both.

They made a path through the dense brush. Marifi felt like her feet were made of stone—she could barely lift her legs to walk. She thought of her grandfather. Would he ever know what became of her? Would he think she ran off and hate her?

The group reached a clearing. The men stopped. The two girls raised their heads to see five heavily armed men in front of them. Were these new men their destination?

But the two groups of men did not seem to have expected each other. The men did not seem to like each other, either. Both gruff groups began to yell. Marifi recognized the uniforms of the new arrivals, if you could call them uniforms. They were with MILF.

She did not know which group would be worse. The drunken criminals might rape and murder them. The terrorists might make them child brides or behead them.

One of the five men commanded, "Drunken infidel, pig-eater. Give us your guns and your girls and go!"

"This is my country, go back south to your islands, you Muslim filth," responded one of the three captors.

No more words were exchanged. Only bullets.

The first shot rang out. Both girls ran into the jungle as fast and as far as they could. The exchange of gunfire increased and the girls huddled behind a thick tree trunk and prayed. They prayed and cried and prayed some more. The minutes felt like hours. Then the shooting stopped. They stayed put and listened, but neither side seemed to be searching for them.

After some time, they chose to emerge from their hiding spot. There were no sounds of men walking through the brush. Nobody yelling for them. Could the men have moved on?

The two girls had to backtrack towards the makeshift town in order to go home. They came to the clearing, the scene of the confrontation, and found eight dead men. They had all killed each other.

It seemed some prayers really are answered.

Marifi rummaged through the dead men's pockets, pulling out what money she could find.

Gina pleaded. "What are you doing? They're dead, that is a sin."

Marifi found the man who had been holding her Golok and pulled it out of his dead hands. "We need the money, go through their pockets, take what you can, hurry," Marifi commanded.

Gina reluctantly reached down to the dead man closest to her and dug into his pocket. She removed several coins, and as she held them up to count, a bloody hand grabbed her wrist.

She screamed and Marifi shushed her as loud as she could. There might be more men coming, if not drawn by the gunfire, they would be drawn to a girl's screams.

Gina continued screaming as the dying man held his grip on her arm.

Marifi slammed her Golok into the prone man's skull. It took only one strike to still him, but Marifi swung the blade down again for good measure, splitting his skull in two like a coconut.

Gina stood there, shocked and silent.

Marifi went through the pockets of the remaining men, relieving them of what money they had. She took only money, no personal belongings, nor guns, as she realized if the guns were missing, people would come looking for the culprits.

As the two girls reached the town, Gina offered Marifi the money she had removed from the dying man.

Marifi refused. "It's yours, keep it."

"I don't want it!" Gina cried, throwing it at Marifi's feet and running off.

Marifi realized then that their brief friendship was over.

She walked over to the shopkeeper woman who had again opened her window for business.

"Give me a soda!" She told the fat lady.

The woman, surprised to see her back, alive, said, "You have no money."

Marifi threw 100 pesos at the fat woman.

The woman looked down, and saw the blood and gore on the blade of her large knife. She quickly handed Marifi a soda, then another. "They are only 50 pesos each," the woman said as she handed the girl a wrapped rice cake. "For you," she said. "For you to eat." The lady spoke with some fear as if Marifi was suddenly to be respected.

Marifi took the soda, the cake, and she made her way back to her grandfather.

It was time to move along again.

37
GOODBYE, DR. ZED

Walter pulled up to the private garage of his office and rolled down the driver's side window to punch in the five-digit code that opened the garage door. When the barrier lifted, he drove forward into the underground parking structure. He noticed that there were fewer cars in the lot than yesterday, and yesterday had fewer cars than the day before.

The curfew was lifted during daylight hours, and this area had been cleared of the infected, so people shouldn't feel apprehensive about coming back to work, but it seemed they did. It seemed that Jersey would become the nation's leader in telecommuting, though he did also notice fewer emails and calls during his workday as well.

Walter parked in the first empty spot on his left. He was not sure why he chose to park right next to the last parked car in the row. The entire garage was available to him, but subconsciously, he fell into the natural progression of filling the next available slot.

He did not get out of his car right away. He chose to finish his coffee and listen to the Infected Update Report on the radio.

The announcer stated that a large horde of assembled infected was making its way towards his area, but it was not expected to arrive for at least another twelve to sixteen hours. The horde was thought to be 300 to 600 strong, but crowd reduction methods were underway.

The announcer continued the broadcast by stating that authorities were advising all residents remain in their homes after 5pm that evening, and to take proper precautions prior to the horde's arrival.

Much like before a snowstorm, residents were asked to avoid travel, keep the roads clear, to stock up on food, water, prescription medicines, and to have Go-Bags ready with additional supplies, cash, flashlights, and copies of essential records should evacuations be mandated.

The announcer reminded residents that they were not to attempt to clear their own yards of infected that might gather, but to wait for authorities to arrive and remove them.

Residents were to stay indoors with windows closed and locked. Should there be a breach of home perimeter by infected, residents were to have a safe room within the home equipped with cellular and landline phone, computer, food, water, and radio. Residents were to hang white towels out of windows to alert authorities of home invasion and wait until security officials arrived.

Residents were advised not to attempt to assist neighbors, or to conduct vigilante attempts to clear one's own neighborhood. Only uniformed PCRC Security Agents were to conduct area clearings.

The announcer was from the overnight shift. Walter was there to relieve him and provide the broadcast announcements for the day shift. Walter worked for Westmore Marketing, which was contracted by PCRC to edit, record, and broadcast the Dr. Zed Infected Update Report on all NJ radio networks. The copy he read on air changed every day. He was the voice of thousands of past political campaign commercials, state fair announcements, and department of transportation updates for road work projects, and now, he reported the movement of zombie hordes as if they were approaching snowstorms. It seemed the natural progression of his career.

Walter looked at his watch. It was 9:15am. He determined he would need to leave work a bit early today if he was to have enough time to hit the market before the expected horde arrival. He probably had more time than he anticipated, as the reports they give him to read were never very accurate.

He rode the elevator to the fifth floor, enjoying the silent company of two others on the ride up. As the doors opened on his floor, and he stepped out, he wondered if he should wish them a good day. He didn't know them, had not said hello to them when he entered. Should he say goodbye as he left? *What was the proper protocol for elevator meetings,* he thought to himself. Before he came to a decision, the door had closed and they were gone. He decided that if he saw them in the elevator tomorrow he would tell them goodbye.

He entered the office and encountered people he knew. Some he had worked with for over fifteen years. Today, as was the case yesterday, people seemed to walk the halls in a trance. He saw Tracy, who was holding a stack of papers she had just picked up from the printer. She stood with her back to the large corporate Xerox, staring off into space, completely lost in thought. The papers in her hand were poorly collated, as if she had already dropped them, then scooped up the scattered stationary, and just held them without squaring the edges. He said, "Good morning," and she gave a startled jump and gasp. She quietly apologized to him for her reaction and rushed off. He had announced an update yesterday that stated that as much as 70% of the state of Jersey could be suffering from PTSD, but those reports were probably not very accurate.

Little was.

He walked past his coworker's offices on the way to his own and it appeared as if many folks had come in just to leave. They were picking up laptops, files, chargers. Some were packing personal items, such as their child's drawings, which had been thumbtacked to the wall, or family photos from the desk. They seemed to be expecting an extended telecommute period.

He made it to the small studio where he would spend his day receiving, editing, and reading copy on the infected movements. He would announce updates about what areas had been overrun and what areas had been cleared, and helpful hints and advice for protecting yourself when infected were moving *en masse* into your neighborhood.

Upon returning from lunch, the number of cars in the garage had decreased. The Infected Update Report copy he received and recited over the air stuck to its original predictions of an arrival between 9:00pm and midnight, but it also said that PCRC Security Force attempts at culling of the numbers was unsuccessful. New reports expected a volume of at least 600 infected, but other estimates stated that the number could grow as high as 1,000 infected arriving by midnight.

The remaining people on his floor were now all heading home to hunker down. He was in no rush as he was used to being the last person in the office after his shift, especially during holidays. He was single with no kids, so people just expected him to bite the bullet and continue to work while those with families headed out early on Thanksgiving and Christmas. He would stay behind and man the phones, returned the emails, shuffle the paper, lock the doors, and turn out the lights at the end of the day. He knew that eventually he would have a wife and children, but needed to focus on other things right now. They say that finding a spouse after forty is more unlikely than getting hit by lightning, but those claims are never very accurate.

As 5:00pm rolled around, the act of walking out of an empty building towards an empty garage was something with which he had grown comfortable. Well, perhaps not comfortable, but familiar. As the elevator door opened onto the first floor of the garage, he noticed the entrance gates had been left open.

He also saw that there were still many of his coworkers' cars parked. And he realized that he was not going to make it to the market that night.

Those arrival time reports were never very accurate.

38
INSHALLAH

Colonel Tindall gazed out through the window at two Skells that staggered past the front lawn of the central house on the cul-de-sac. He and his men were about to haul ass. He wanted them gone, but he was curious nonetheless. "These things are fascinating," he said to no one in particular.

"They are not things, they are people," Woodrow said.

"Bullshit. They stopped being people once their brain turned to oatmeal and we became the other white meat."

"Speak for yourself," Moz chimed in.

Tindall glanced over at him and smiled—his first real smile since he'd left FOB Prince.

He slung his rucksack over his shoulder, checked his sidearm, and looked back at the assembled soldiers geared up to follow him to the ends of the earth...or to the secret Jersey compound that he was taking them.

There was also one overweight former night watchman looking to recreate himself.

Tindall looked to Moz. "Last chance, dark meat."

Moz smiled. "Thank you, colonel. I'll take my chances here, *Inshallah*."

Dr. Moz found Woodrow's tale of GRASS and the broadcast they were forcing him into dubious, at best. He was equally distrusting of GRASS's motives, but decided to stick it out with Woodrow...for the time being.

Moz was born to an Indian mother and an Egyptian father. They had toiled as laborers in the United Arab Emirates, which was one of the better places to actually live and grow up.

His father arrived in the UAE in his twenties and followed the routine as most laborers do. He rented a bed in one of the worker camps outside of Abu Dhabi. These were stone barracks, which slept eight to a room. You rented your bed by shift, which meant if you worked during the day, a man who worked during the night slept in your bed during the day. When he woke to go to his evening shift, he would vacate the bed for Moz's father at night.

Buses with no air conditioners shuttled workers back and forth from the camps to the cities all day and night. Small, revolving blade fans churned above every other seat, but usually, only a third of the fans worked. The summers were brutal, with temperatures reaching well above 100 degrees.

That didn't matter. His father laid bricks in the sun, creating beautifully ornate designs on the embankments between the roads. The work was brutal and the conditions were harsh, but he made enough to send back to his family and still survive.

His designs caught the eye of a developer and he was hired to create tile and porcelain frescos in one of the many shopping malls that dotted the city. In that mall, he met a beautiful girl working in a shop that sold souvenirs to tourists: hookah pipes, prayer rugs, and incense burners.

After the sun set, and the cooler night air replaced the stifling heat, Abu Dhabi became magical. They married, and after a couple years sharing an apartment with others, they were able to afford a tiny apartment of their own. In time, they had a single child. He would grow up and be educated in the seemingly only tranquil oasis in a turbulent Middle East.

He inherited his father's eye for design and fell in love with the chemical and biological make up of organisms. He received a scholarship to attend a local university, and afterwards, traveled to Egypt for advanced education. It was there that things took a wrong turn.

Moz and three classmates decided to travel to the resort area of Dahab one Saturday. On their way back, Moz drifted off to sleep in the back seat behind the driver. He awoke to find the car had come to a stop in the middle of an isolated desert road back to Cairo. Four heavily armed men stood guard at a roadblock that was not much more than three steel oil drums placed in the center of the road.

The leader of the men was the only one in uniform, the others looked as though they had come from a night of disco directly to their posts, but with the large AK-47s they were holding, no one would argue their lack of propriety. The leader came over, heavyset, top buttons of his shirt undone to display a generous amount of body hair. He asked the driver for the men's identification. Each of them dutifully handed over their student cards. The driver handed them to one of the casually dressed men, who used his cell phone to call someone and read off each card's information.

The leader looked at the four for a bit, with a hint of disdain at the young, educated men who would someday most likely leave Egypt to make their futures. He told them to get out of the car and they obeyed.

They stood side by side at the car. Moz was nervous, but his three companions had grown up in Egypt, where such harassment by the authorities was a common occurrence. The car's driver whispered to the others that he expected the soldiers to ask them to pay a toll to continue forward. Each smiled as they anticipated this stop as nothing more than a shakedown for a few dollars.

The soldier returned and handed the ID cards to the uniformed leader, he pointed to one of the IDs while leaning towards the uniformed soldier and muttering something in his ear. The soldier told them to get back in the car and be on their way. As they did, and as Moz closed his door, the uniformed man yelled out in anger.

The four men froze.

"You!" He said, pointing at Moz. "You stepped on my foot!"

"No, I did not," he protested, not realizing he had stepped on the man's foot at all.

"You did," said the man, pulling Moz from the car.

"Sir, I did not realize. I assure you it was not on purpose. I apologize."

"You are under arrest for assaulting an officer," the uniformed solder announced.

"What?!" Moz screeched. Fear and shock shook him.

"You three, go, drive on!" The other soldier commanded.

The students attempted to get out of the car, but the guards leveled their guns at them, one shouting, "If you move, you will be shot!"

The three students retreated into the car.

"Now go!" The man in the uniform yelled at them. "You can collect your friend at the Cairo central police department, or you can stay and be arrested as well."

The three had no choice. They gave one last look to Moz's confused and terrified eyes and drove off. Over the horizon. The students immediately reported the incident to the Cairo police, the Egyptian Army, and the university, but not having any identification or even a name as to who the men on the road were, nor even an exact position of where they were stopped, made the effort futile.

Moz was taken to Afghanistan by his captors a few days later. He assumed the soldiers had been told that he, with his chemical engineering and biological research background, would be of value to certain organizations.

The guards had been bribed by the terrorists to be on the lookout for such people, and when found, they would be rewarded for delivering them.

Afghanistan was his home with his new captors for a month before Moz was caught, along with other scientists, by Americans and sent to GITMO, the US prison in Cuba. After a year of captivity, a trade was negotiated. Several prisoners were to be swapped in exchange for some Americans held by the Taliban. Dr. Moz and two other scientists held in the prison were chosen for the exchange. He begged the Americans not to send him back to the Taliban.

Moz had befriended an American soldier who worked at the prison. The two bonded over their mutual love of film and when Moz pleaded with him to not allow the swap, the soldier told him in confidence that there was nothing he could do, that it was being ordered by someone powerful. The soldier told him that an American one-star general in Afghanistan had opposed the exchange, and had complained so loudly that he was demoted to the rank of colonel and reassigned to a place that was supposedly even worse than Kandahar.

A place called Jersey.

The swap went forward anyway, but to Dr. Moz's surprise, he and the other scientists did *not* get sent back to the hands of the Taliban.

No.

They were sent to the New Jersey-based laboratories of PCRC and were put to work on the Modified Embryonic Animal Tissue experiments.

39
ROAD TRIP

Fiona hit every key possible on her laptop trying to get the video connection back with Woodrow. She had no idea how he had accessed her laptop and she had no idea how to reopen the video chat.

She threw her laptop on the bed and ran down the hall to James's room. She was going to insist he take her to Princeton University to try and find where Woodrow was hiding out. She knew James would fight her on this, tell her it was too dangerous, and she would have to make a big show of how if he did not escort her, she would go alone.

She burst into his room to find him sitting at the edge of his hotel bed, facing the bare wall.

"I need you to take me to Princeton University right now. I just received a video from Woodrow saying he was there, but your security teams chased them out and are now hunting him down. I want you to drive me there right now, and if you don't, I'll—"

James rose up from his perch on the bed. "Okay, let's go."

"What?" She blinked. Not sure if he was serious. Even less certain of why it would be that easy.

"I said let's go, I need a change of scenery." He reached over and swiped the car keys from the top of his dresser.

"Okay...thanks."

They made their way down to the garage and took off in James's Humvee.

They drove for almost an hour, silent, with not a word shared between them. Fiona stared out the window at the endless expanse of trees as they navigated the back roads past Wharton State Forrest.

James had stayed off the main roads after seeing several Must Gut Them warnings and a white PCRC containment truck on the side of the road in a strange angle. The back doors were open and the driver's side door was smeared with blood. The scattered body parts strewn around told tale of a containment gone wrong.

"It's metastasizing," James said aloud, but to himself.

"What is?" Fiona asked.

"They can't control this. They think they can, but it is too far gone. It will spread. There is no treatment." He continued to mumble.

She watched him. Worried about his mental state. "I thought they were housing them in quarantine till a cure or treatment could be found."

"Who?"

"The infected. You were just talking about the infected."

James's eyes narrowed. "Yeah, right, them."

She sat silent, looking at him. "Every time I am in the car with you, I am completely lost," she said and returned to watching the trees.

They drove in silence for another couple of miles.

"Look," Fiona yelled. "There's a man up there."

"Probably infected," James said.

"No way, he's too fat. He's waiving us down."

"We ain't stopping."

"We need to help him!" Fiona pleaded.

"No, no way, we are not helping anyone, and we are not picking up strangers."

"You need to pull over."

As they approached the portly man waving his arms in distress, Fiona grabbed the steering wheel and forced an angry James to pull the car to the side of the road.

The man started to walk up to the car, but then stopped, turned, and ran into the woods.

Six men in military uniforms emerged and surrounded the car.

James looked at Fiona, but she was too scared to return his glare.

The men pointed assault rifles at the car. A tense minute passed and then a new man emerged from the woods. The portly guy followed him a few feet behind.

"Hello, sir, ma'am," the man said as politely as possible. "I truly apologize for this inconvenience, but we are going to have to confiscate your vehicle. We will not harm you and we won't take any of your personal belongings, we just need the vehicle. We will drive you to a safe zone and ensure you arrive there unharmed."

Fiona sneered. "Why? We're not breaking curfew."

"I did not say you were. I am just saying we need to commandeer your vehicle for ourselves."

"Do you work for PCRC?" She demanded.

"No, ma'am, we do not."

"Well, my friend here is a senior executive at PCRC, and they manage all the security for this state."

James shot her a death-stare, realizing she just blew any chance they had of getting out of there without a fight.

"*Oooh* really." The man looked off to some unknown authority. "We have a PCRC contractor." Then back at James and Fiona. "Sir, can I ask you if you are currently armed?"

James said nothing.

"Sir, I am asking you—"

"I heard you. I am not armed," James said reluctantly.

"Well, that is a surprise, as I have never, and I mean *never*, met a PCRC contractor who was not armed. Could you do me a favor and pop the trunk?"

"Why don't you tell me who you are and what you want first."

"Sir, my name is Colonel James Tindall, and these here are my men, and what I want is for you to pop the trunk."

One of the soldiers raised his gun slightly higher to put James's forehead directly in his crosshairs.

James reached down and pulled the latch to the trunk. A *clunk* sounded from behind. One of the soldiers walked over and looked in.

"Holy shit!"

"Sergeant!" Colonel Tindall scolded. "There is a lady present, watch your language!"

"Sorry, sir. There's a whole arsenal back here." The sergeant picked up and put down high-powered assault rifles, handguns, explosive charges, and boxes of ammo.

"Sir, ma'am, I apologize for my man's coarse language, but if you don't mind, I think you two better come with us for a bit. Our camp isn't far from here, and I assure you, you will be safe and protected."

40
WANDERING JEW

0303 pondered the glass of whiskey he cradled in his hands. His ex-wife would have loved to see him like this, day drinking in a dive bar. He hated her even though he didn't remember why, couldn't recall when that hatred began.

He knew there must have been a beginning at the same that he knew he loved her at one time. A time before they were always angry at each other. Maybe it was because he was a simple man and anger was also simple. Easy. It was so easy to snipe at each other, identify reasons to criticize, or point out something the other did wrong. It was easy and he was lazy.

Forgiveness was difficult.

Apologies opened up vulnerabilities that could be later exploited.

Cynicism was easy too.

It was so easy to get lost in dark thoughts of regrets, of insults and slights, be they real or imagined. Those dark thoughts moved in a perpetual spiral on their own power. They would not gain or lose momentum. They just kept going and going and going at a steady, soul-crushing pace. Ceasing these dark, angry thoughts required work and effort. Ah! That was energy he chose not to expend. He'd rather leave his demons alone to feed.

The bar was populated by other similarly angry people.

Angry they couldn't go to work. Angry they couldn't apply their trade. Angry they couldn't make a living due to the Skells. Angry they felt helpless to stop the growing population of *new* Skells. Angry they no longer felt safe in their own neighborhoods, their homes. Angry they were stuck in New Jersey while news crews stood just outside the borders reporting as if it were now a leper colony full of diseased creatures that should never be let out.

Yet the narrative they heard on television and the radio was now compassionate bullshit.

Feel for the Skells, for they cannot help what they do. Feel for the Skells, for they do not know what they do.

The outside narrative was to be humane in rounding them up and housing them till a cure could be found.

Jersey's working class wasn't without sympathy for the Skells. They knew they were human beings. Or used to be human beings. Perhaps they still were. But there were too many of them. Violent. Dangerous. And their numbers were growing.

Humanitarianism could call in the future, once there was a better hold on the situation. Once more was known about them and how to deal with them. But right now, something needed to be done to contain them. To eradicate the threat.

Something needed to be done.

Ivan and Marifi walked through the door of The Shore Thing bar, holding it open just long enough for the light to shine directly onto the corner booth occupied by 0303.

He squinted at the light until the door closed and his eyes adjusted, recognizing Ivan.

"Well, well, look who's here," 0303 spat out. "Someone must have chanted Beetle-*Jew* three times for you to appear."

Ivan ignored the anti-Semitic taunt, walked over to the booth, and sat down across from 0303. Marifi positioned herself on a barstool facing the door they just entered.

0303 lifted his whiskey. "So, the prodigal son returns. Want a drink? Might be your last."

"Accepting wine from Judas, not likely Banko." Ivan responded, using Bankowski's high school bully nickname.

0303 sneered. "You may be a Jew, but you ain't Jesus, and your dad ain't God. Besides, I don't have to poison you. When I kill you, I'll do it with my bare hands."

"Threatening the boss's son. Not the path for a promotion," Ivan replied.

"I don't give a fuck what you think, asswipe. You're lucky I'm off-duty, otherwise I would arrest your ass. Your daddy ain't here to protect you, boy."

"I know. That's why I brought my wife." Ivan kept an even, condescending tone.

"Wife!" 0303 laughed. "Is that what you still call her? Just a mutt your daddy brought home from the pound to keep his loser son company."

"Okay, well, it was nice catching up." Ivan flipped 0303 the bird with both hands. "But let's cut to the chase. What I need from you is your PCRC electronic ID card so I can get into the hotel that houses my dad and our new young president."

0303 let out a loud chortle. "Yeah, right!" He leaned forward in the booth. "Why don't you just reach over and take it?"

"Banko, I am going—"

"Going to what?" He interrupted. "What? You gonna sic your chink wife on me?"

Ivan adjusted himself in his seat and displayed a .38 in his waistband.

Another loud laugh burst forth from 0303. "You brought a fucking revolver to a gun fight? You're worse than your fucking 'wife' with her knife. She gonna cut me with her little sword?" He pointed to Marifi's Golok. "How about I take it from her and carve my initials in your forehead?"

"My wife would slice open your nutsack before you got half way over there."

Marifi did not look at them, but she listened to every word, and it surprised her how good it felt to hear Ivan refer to her as his wife.

"Maybe I should go over there and give her *my* sword," 0303 threatened, grabbing his crotch. "I would split that little whore in half."

Ivan sighed. "I was hoping this would go so much better."

"Gold, get the fuck out of here before you both come down with a case of dead."

"Okay." Ivan held up his hands in mock surrender. "I did try to reason with you." He stood and walked towards the door.

"Oh, and Ivan," 0303 called after him. "When the order comes down to kill you, it's not gonna be your wife who does it, it's gonna be me."

Ivan turned around and stormed back to 0303. "How are you going to do that when you're in quarantine?" Ivan enacted the only fight move he had ever learned and gave a swift kick to his opponent's balls, bringing 0303 to his knees, groaning in pain.

"This man has been infected!" Ivan yelled. "He tried to bite me!"

The bar patrons sprang to action and grabbed brooms, bar stools, and anything else they could find. They wailed on the crouching, cursing man.

Marifi reached into the scrum and sliced the cord to 0303's PCRC contractor ID, which provided access to all facilities.

She tossed it to Ivan and the two ran out the door.

41

WELCOME TO NUKE JERSEY

Woodrow spoke into the laptop microphone. He hoped the audience would be receptive. "My name is Dr. Woodrow Coleman. I am an author and a scientist. What you are seeing right now is not a hoax. This is live footage from inside the quarantine zones of New Jersey."

Website and television monitors around the globe displayed eight video feeds side by side, each in a box as if watching the beginning of *The Brady Bunch*. Instead of displaying the smiling faces of that extended, incestuous family, each box displayed a different security camera from quarantine camps and depopulation facilities around the state. The feeds changed every thirty seconds to show different angles the Skell slaughtering activities that took place.

GRASS was now fully in control of Colonel Tindall's laptop. As soon as Woodrow had powered it on and the computer connected to the web, GRASS took control. They searched through the code of all loaded applications for what they were really after.

Patrick sat in his presidential office in Cape May, watching the broadcast, along with much of the rest of the United States.

"How is he doing this?" President Callahan demanded of his aides in the room.

"Sir, he somehow got access to a private signal the military has control over should there be a need to communicate with the country during a national emergency."

Patrick pointed to the screen displaying Skells suffocating in foam. "Is this real? Is this happening? Have we sanctioned this?"

Woodrow continued, "The infected are not being housed until a cure can be found, they are being slaughtered in a process called depopulation. They are being suffocated and their remains are being carted out as medical waste to be incinerated."

The cameras showed scenes of infected struggling against the foam, appearing to shriek and suffer. Other cameras showed more queued up for entry into depopulation chambers. Other cameras showed trucks marked "PCRC Biohazard Transport" leaving camps.

What viewers did not see was that GRASS had found the application they were looking for on Tindall's laptop.

Woodrow talked over the ever-switching images. "It is my belief that our new president was unaware of this activity and I know he would never allow this to occur. I hope he's watching this so that he can put a stop to this barbarity."

Woodrow took a deep breath.

"I know these people, the poor infected, seem scary. I know the first thought is to destroy them. We often want to destroy what we fear or don't understand. I myself destroyed a group of infected when I didn't understand what was truly happening."

Woodrow thought back to the PCRC lab. How he had melted dozens of Skells by releasing a shower of thermite on them before he fled the building.

Woodrow pleaded with his invisible listening audience. "We don't need to do this; these are not monsters. They are infected. They are evolving and changing in ways we don't know, but we can stop the spread. We can even possibly reverse the process for those exposed. I was the one whose ideas caused this to happen. Please allow me the time to set things right. Skells are people!"

The cameras showed bulldozers being driven by men in hazmat suits pushing the remains of the infected into large bins, which were then sealed and loaded into trucks. Occasionally, an infected would start to stagger up, not yet dead. Other workers in black tactical outfits and gas masks would walk over and slice open the survivor's midsection, causing internal organs and the stomach to fall to the ground. Sometimes the men would need to cut the remaining intestines to get the stomach completely separated. Sometimes they would stomp on or kick the fallen stomach to ensure it was destroyed.

What the watchers did not see was the GRASS Cyber Army preparing their closing remarks.

42
DEAD LIVES MATTER

"Thank you, Dr. Woody, your services will no longer be needed," came the electronic voice.

Woodrow pushed several buttons on the keyboard. He no longer had any control of the laptop.

The voice spoke. Digitized. Deep. Menacing. "I would now like to address the American sheeple. I am speaking on behalf of the Blades of GRASS. As grass feeds the sheep, the GRASS movement will spoon feed you sheeple."

"Fear not America, the zombie apocalypse will not bring about the end. Because the trough-feeding pigs of our government are the real living dead. The sign of the devil is not marked by three sixes. It is marked by the three evil entities that comprise the government, military, and commercial complex. This unholy trinity can't be killed—it can only be restrained. Like the arsonist firefighter, the government perpetuates its own purpose. It exists to exist.

"It is no different than the zombie hordes who will soon be consuming their way through your cities. The government will continue moving forward, eternally consuming, exponentially increasing in size and hunger. The government cannot innovate, it can only replicate.

"We, the Blades of GRASS, have given you the gift of opportunity.

"For too long, Americans have ignored the world. America is a country founded on racism, oppression, colonialism, and greed. For too long we have meddled in the world's affairs, imposing our will. This time, the Blades of GRASS will cut you down to size.

"What you are seeing on the screen right now are live feeds from the slaughter houses set up by your government, through their proxy Post Conflict Restoration Corp. Soon, they will not need their hired guns. Soon they will have their own undead army. An army created of VINNI's"

The screens on thousands—possibly millions—of televisions, computers, and phones displayed footage of Skells going through de-pop. They struggled against the rising tide of foam, shrieking and clawing at each other.

The GRASShole resumed his speech. "PCRC unleashed the virus and now is paid to clean it up. And who is the surrogate son of the founder and CEO of PCRC? None other than our newly installed President Patrick Callahan. How convenient.

"And who gave birth to the virus that was unleashed? None other than our president's childhood friend: author, health guru, and father of the apocalypse, Dr. Woodrow

Coleman. Here are the emails he had written explaining his actions."

On the screen, copies of Woodrow's emails appeared. He had written them, but never sent a single one. Some were still in his draft folder and some had been deleted long ago.

"*Tsk tsk*, Dr. Coleman," the voice scolded. "Don't you know better than to use a private server to share emails with sensitive information? That is just *dumb*!

"Now, I am not one to bring up a lot of problems without having at least one solution. New Jersey has become a cancer. Usually a cancer is treated with chemicals and radiation. The chemicals have had no effect, so now we will try radiation.

"We have taken control of the missile silos at FE Warren Air Force Base. We will be launching those missiles directly into the heart of New Jersey."

Back at the Congress Hotel, staffers watched in disbelief.

"What? What did he just say?!" President Callahan yelled at the advisors who had gathered in his office to watch the broadcast. "Our own nuclear weapons are about to be launched? Is that fucking possible?"

"Is *this* possible?" Spencer pointed to the screens displaying the pirate broadcast. "If they can hijack our communications system, there's no telling what else they can do."

"Well, we need to stop it. Get the base on the phone, shut the missiles down," Patrick ordered.

"We can try, but if the system has been hacked, we won't get control of it." Spencer's hands shook. He was losing it. Fear took hold.

Maxwell Gold walked into the room. "What the hell is happening?"

Spencer spoke up again. "It could have been a virus that was inserted as a software update when this idiot started broadcasting."

"A software update, how the hell does our nuclear arsenal get a virus?" Maxwell demanded.

"It's software, it acts like any other software. It has updates just like every other application. They found a back door, a vulnerability, either this guy broadcasting knew about it, or they tricked him into giving them access."

Maxwell yelled at the room. "Christ almighty. Shut the entire system down!"

Two large PCRC Security Team members ran in. They flanked Patrick. "Sir, you are the leader of this country, we need to get you to a secure location right now."

"*Okay,*" Patrick and Maxwell said in unison, each assuming he was the leader being referenced. They then awkwardly looked at each other, as did the security men.

The two men grabbed Patrick's arms and began leading him out of the office with Maxwell and Spencer jogging close behind.

"We have no bomb shelter here, but there is a large walk-in freezer in the basement. It's the best bet. Keep moving," said the contractor holding Patrick's right arm.

Patrick was brought down the hallway, and then down a flight of steps to the basement. His feet barely touched the ground.

Another said to Maxwell Gold, "Sir, we need to keep up!"

Maxwell cocked his eye at the merc. "No shit."

The group of men made it to the large freezer. The door was open. The cooling portion had been turned off, but the large steel door and walls were satisfactory for a temporary bunker.

All of the men's phones began to beep together.

Dr. Reynolds ran down the stairs. "Sir, people are fleeing their homes, trying to get out of the state. It's bedlam out there."

"If they can launch a missile at us, how much time do we have?" Patrick demanded.

"Dr. Reynolds?" Spencer asked.

Dr. Reynolds opened her binder and pulled out a calculator. "The Minuteman III missile has an advertised velocity of about 28,000 kilometers per hour, or roughly 300 miles per minute. Warren AFB, where this missile has been launched from, is about 1,800 miles from us. As these missiles are designed to fly halfway around a curved earth, a flat-earth parabolic trajectory calculation would require a low launch. Warren is at an altitude of 6,129 feet above sea level while New Jersey is basically at sea level.

"Now...this is where the complications set in, as atmospheric air resistance plus the initial launch acceleration time could add a few seconds to the total time...the actual time of flight may be a few seconds shorter or longer."

Spencer's eyes rolled around in his head. "How fucking long? Just tell us, you crazy bitch!"

"Six minutes," came the despondent response.

"Six fucking minutes?" Patrick asked.

"Well, closer to four now," Dr. Reynolds said.

"Go! Get him in the bunker now," shouted the security contractor.

"We need to get him on a plane or a copter, get him out of the *state*," Spencer responded.

"No time," the other contractor said.

"We need to alert the people. We need to warn people," Patrick pleaded.

"No *time*, they wouldn't be able to do anything anyway. Other than kiss their asses goodbye."

Upstairs, word had spread throughout the Congress Hotel. Workers, contractors, security guards, and aides fled the building through the doors and even windows. They raced to get somewhere, anywhere, else.

Protesters and the media who had been camped outside the hotel since Patrick's inauguration saw the mass exodus, and although they did not know why the new president's staff was fleeing the building, they decided it was not wise to stick around.

They too fled.

On the broadcast, the cow head of GRASS continued his rant: "As for the rest of the country, what you are seeing on your screens right now is heading your way. "

GRASS set phase two in motion.

Truth told, they did not have the ability to launch any missiles, but using Tindall's laptop, they were able to hack into the master control switch of all Kraken systems. With a few keystrokes, the sound machines that had kept the Skells calm and contained went silent.

The cow continued: "We have shut down the sound systems that have been keeping the infected compliant, and now we will shut down the systems that have kept *you* compliant. The infected are now free to leave the confines of the state of New Jersey. All of America shall soon be united, with man and Skell living, and dying, side by side.

"There are no politicians to turn to anymore, America, so take advantage of this crisis, this opportunity, this chance for a new way of doing things.

"Your future will either be in your own hands, or in their stomachs.

"We are the Blades of GRASS, and we are sprouting everywhere."

The voiceover message from GRASS stopped.

The video feeds now showed the Skells free, wild, and attacking workers at the camp. The view switched between camera shots to display various scenes of horror. Kraken sound systems were systematically turned off. Skells ran rampant. They slaughtered their way out of the containment camps.

More camera feeds appeared on the screen. PCRC Security Teams fled and got devoured while firing their weapons at the hordes of bloody, skeletal creatures in the streets.

GRASS's plan was diabolically perfect. It released the infected and then drove the uninfected out of their homes in a mad dash for the border, only to be greeted by hungry Skells.

The cameras changed again to display video from bridges and tunnels leading out of New Jersey. Panicked citizens tried to escape nuclear annihilation, but they ended up in the arms and mouths of freed Skells. Both infected and uninfected alike overran the National Guard and police officers posted in neighboring states.

It was an orgy of panic, fear, and brutality.

43

FINGERED

The chaos on the streets provided cover for Big V, now a mere wisp of himself, to slip free from his hideout and make his way to the Sullivan beach house. He found it empty, as expected. He found the safe behind the picture in the pool room, also empty, which meant Ragu had followed his orders. He had hoped that Ragu would have left some of the cash behind for him, as he requested, should he survive, but no such luck. Ragu learned well: Never leave cash on the table.

V rummaged through the bar fridge, but found nothing that looked appealing. In fact, since he survived the Skell virus, he, a man with enormous appetites, had not felt the urge to eat at all. While he did not crave human flesh like the other infected. He did not crave his pre-virus favorites of gabagool, ossobuco, or any type of bread or cheese ever created. He even walked past a cannoli store without an issue.

Watching him secretly from the walk-in closet was Gary Ragu.

He hadn't seen his former boss since before the outbreak, and while V had lost a preposterous amount of weight, his mannerisms were the same.

Ragu thought back to the first time he had seen Big V. Ragu had been a street thug, unaffiliated with any of the families, his only loyalty was to heroin, and his only friend was a violent junkie name Ramirez. The two of them had jumped three couples who were leaving a fancy restaurant. Ramirez beat two of the guys up pretty badly, even though they put up no real resistance. He and Ramirez then had spent the next two hours looking all over for heroin, but could only score Oxycodone. They crushed it up and were about to partake when the door to their pathetic drug den was kicked in.

What they thought were cops rushed them and they were dragged out.

When they were thrown in the trunk of a Lexus, they realized their captors were not cops.

They were taken to a warehouse where several large men gathered. One of the women they had jumped earlier was also there. Turned out she was the sister of one of V's top guys.

After she confirmed who they were, she was escorted out, obviously not to witness the bloodshed that was going to follow.

Ragu looked over at Ramirez. The guy shook like a leaf. He did not know if it was fear or withdrawal.

"You guys are actually here on a good night," V stated as he walked out of the darkness. "I am looking for some new guys, some tough guys. And I am going to allow you to *wow* me."

Ramirez spoke first. "You...you're not going to kill us?"

Fucking idiot! Gary thought.

"Should I?" V responded. "How about this. I am going to give you a choice. You work for me. You bring me 100% of what you bring in, and I will give you back what percentage I feel you deserve. I will do this until I feel your debt to me is paid. How does that sound?"

"So we join you or you kill us?" Ramirez sputtered.

"When life's major decisions come your way," V said, taking a slow, philosophical tone, "You always have three choices to make. Yes... No... Or wait."

They all stood in silence for a good sixty seconds.

V quickly drew a gun from his belt and pointed it directly at Ramirez's face.

"Wait!" Ramirez yelled, holding up his hands.

V shot him in the head and his body slumped to the ground.

V turned to Ragu. "He chose 'wait.' That was the wrong answer. Of course, 'no' would have been wrong too."

"Yes!" Ragu said, trying not to show any fear. "Yes."

V realized he was not alone.

"You look good," Ragu said. "I don't think you were this thin in high school."

Big V stood up and slowly turned around, making no sudden movements. He figured Ragu was not here to reminisce. He faced Ragu, who was pointing a 9mm at him. "I wasn't. Funny thing happened to me on my way to the shore."

"How long?" Ragu asked, referring to his boss being an informant.

"Does it matter?"

"Guess not. Want to tell me why?" Ragu still had some sentiment for his old mentor and friend.

"I know this won't really change things, but it was not about you guys," V explained. "The feds didn't give a shit about dealing prescription meds and running games from the back of the strip club. They were after Maxwell Gold and his company. I got pinched. I made a deal. Not trying to justify my actions, but it is what it is."

"I guess it is what it is." Ragu repeated.

"You talk to Schaffer?" V asked, referring to his FBI handler. V had advised Ragu to make a deal with the fed and offer up all of V's recordings as barter to get out of Jersey alive.

"I did. I turned down his offer and went another route," said Ragu.

"Let me guess, you get your membership card back, but you have to kill me, right?"

"Like you said, it is what it is."

"They want proof?" V asked.

Ragu nodded the affirmative.

"They say anything they wanted in specific?" V asked.

Ragu shook his head.

Big V reached into his pocket and pulled out a baggie containing a severed finger. He tossed the bag to Ragu.

"The wife bit it off me. She turned into one of those things. I kept it on ice at this custard place over on the boardwalk, so it ain't that shriveled. It still looks almost fresh. I know I'm asking a lot, but that is your proof. You don't need to do this. I just want to see my daughter."

Ragu shook the bag holding the finger. "If you turn up, they'll know I lied, and I'll be dead."

V nodded. "True, but I won't be turning up. I'll be vapor. I know you don't trust me anymore, but I promise you, I won't be seen again."

The two men stood there in silence while Ragu contemplated. He took a deep breath, turned around and as he was leaving the basement, he directed his first command as the new boss of the New Jersey family towards Big V: "Vaper."

44
EVERY MAN FOR HIMSELF

"Wait, wait!" Dr. Reynolds yelled out, a cell phone pressed to her ear. "It's a hoax. I'm on the phone with Warren airbase right now. They say there has been no hack and no missiles are being launched!"

"What the hell is going on?" Patrick demanded.

"We don't know, sir," Spencer said. "But right now, the safest place for us, I mean, for *you*, is in the freezer, err...presidential bunker."

"He's correct." Dr. Reynolds chimed in. "The technical team has been working on this space as a safe room in case of emergency for the past two days. We have communications, power, food, everything we need to be safe until we figure out what is happening. We need to secure the president!"

At that, Patrick was hustled into the freezer, with Spencer and Reynolds rushing in as if boarding the last lifeboat on the Titanic.

Maxwell turned to one of the security contractors "You, come with me!"

"You're not staying?" Patrick asked.

"No, I am an old man. As long as you're secured, I am fine."

Patrick stepped forward as if to follow.

Maxwell turned to Spencer and barked: "You! You seal this door now, and you keep the president and Dr. Reynolds inside and safe until you hear from me or you are sure the situation is one hundred percent safe. Do you understand your orders?"

Spencer stood as straight and tall as his weak spine would allow. "Yes, sir!" He gave his freezer mates a nervous look, then pulled the large door closed and sealed it from inside.

Outside the bunker, unaware that it was a hoax, the word was still spreading that an inbound nuclear missile was heading towards the Jersey Shore. Just like any other Sunday night, people were fleeing the area in all directions, trying to get as far north as possible, leaving the Congress Hotel and Executive Office abandoned except for a few dozen Skells that were now free and roaming the halls.

Inside the freezer/bunker, it was silent as a grave. The sound of the three breathing was the only noise. Patrick walked over to a small wooden desk and chair in the corner and put his head in his hands. Spencer surveyed the supplies and electronic equipment that had been installed. Dr. Reynolds stood stoic.

"Sir, may I talk to you about something?" she said to Patrick.

He raised his head.

Spencer turned around nervously.

Patrick said, "Of course."

"I think the president has had enough for the day and needs some quiet contemplation time," Spencer said to the doctor.

Dr. Reynolds ignored Spencer and addressed Patrick. "Sir, you need to know exactly what—"

"That is enough, Reynolds!" Spencer snapped.

"No, it's not enough, he needs to know," She countered.

"I need to know what?" Patrick asked.

"Nothing, you need to know nothing!" Spencer yelled. He realized he was shouting at the president and took a conciliatory tone. "I am sorry, sir, it's just that there is a time and a place, and now and here are not that time and place."

"When?" Reynolds asked. "I am...he needs to know! He's the president!"

"I said *enough!*" Spencer yelled, walking over and getting in Reynolds's face. He bent over so that his mug was an inch from hers. "Now is *not* the time, here is *not* the place and he is *not* in charge!" Spencer yelled at her while pointing at Patrick. "Do you get that, you—"

Dr. Reynolds swung up her right hand, palm out, and slammed Spencer in the nose. His nostrils exploded and blood erupted through his fingers as he cradled his broken schnozz.

"That's for calling me a dumb bitch!" She shouted at the whimpering man. She turned to a stunned, silent Patrick, adjusted her glasses, and took the chair next to him.

She began telling Patrick a horrific tale in which he was the unwitting star.

45
REVANCHIST

Maxwell walked back to his office. A security contractor followed closely behind, keeping an eye out for any roaming Skells or crazed protesters who would use this opportunity to try and storm the place. The guard spotted neither. The entire hotel had been abandoned.

Maxwell arrived at his office door and turned to the contractor. "I need to get things straightened out. I need to restore calm. I need *you* to guard this door and not let anyone bother me. No one enters this office, not even you, is that understood?"

"Yes, sir," he replied. He assumed a guard position just right of the door.

Maxwell entered and closed the door behind him. He looked down at the ground and took a long, exasperated breath. "Let's keep that arrogant little prick in the cooler for a while." He muttered referring to Patrick, his proxy president.

"Talking to yourself...that is the first sign of madness," said a voice behind him.

Maxwell spun around. Someone was in the chair facing his desk. He could not see who, but the arrogant bastard had his feet up on the coffee table.

"Zombie apocalypse not going as planned? Shame that everything you give birth to turns out to be such a disappointment."

"Ivan?" Maxwell asked as he approached his desk and saw his son sitting in the chair. It had been so long since he had seen him in person that it took him a moment to recognize his own kin. Maxwell then noticed Marifi standing in the corner of the room. He eyed her warily.

Ivan said, "Don't worry, dad, she's not going to kill either of us. At least not today."

"What do you want?" Maxwell asked, sitting down at his desk.

"What does any kid want? I'm here to collect my allowance." Ivan's voice dripped with venom and snark.

"What do you *want*, Ivan?" Maxwell was getting irritated.

Ivan looked over at Marifi. "Notice how I called him dad and he called me Ivan. Not 'son.' These petty micro-aggressions. Yes, that was what my shrink called it. Micro-aggressions. You know, I don't think I received enough affection as a child. What do you think, my dear?"

She shrugged. She acted unconcerned, but she knew Ivan had been off his meds since they fled the bunker. He had been taking prescribed antidepressants, anti-OCD, and sleeping pills, but the meds were all blown up along with their home almost a week ago. He was getting twitchy.

Ivan bent over and reached into his backpack on the floor. Maxwell tensed up and began reaching for his right desk drawer, where he kept his gun.

Ivan raised back up and tossed a hardcover notebook onto the desk. "Dr. Coleman's journal. I found it in your old building. By the way, this one is much nicer. Not as burnt up."

"I am going to ask you one last time. What do you want?" Maxwell said, raising his voice on the word "want" in the hopes that the security guard might come in to check on him. Unfortunately, his guards follow orders very well.

Ivan leaned forward in his chair. "I have spent the last several years digging holes in the ground. Some of which I even lived in. Some of which were for other people to live in. Some of which had different purposes. So, you ask me, what do I want, you ask? Hmm. Where to begin?"

46
THE HIVE

TransWays Depot, nicknamed The Hive, was the largest trucking warehouse in southern Jersey. Located just off the turnpike, it boasted fifty truck loading bays on one side and an additional fifty on the other. The single story facility could handle the delivery, storage, turnaround, and release of hundreds of tons of freight. It was the perfect facility for the largest cleanup operation undertaken in New Jersey since Hurricane Sandy.

The facility had needed some configuration, but not much. Large highway barrier walls—usually installed to keep sound inside the roadways—were set up around the facility to keep prying eyes out.

The operation was straightforward. As long as the infected continued to hear the hum, they were a dangerous, but docile cargo. PCRC Containment Teams would travel around the state, corralling the infected into the trucks, which brought them to The Hive, where they were held until depopulation foaming could occur.

While the foaming of smaller groups was being conducted at the Q Camps, the bulk of the work was coming to The Hive now that the facility was operational. Trucks were backed into the bay at the front of the building, and the hazardous cargo was coaxed to shamble out into the main holding facility of the warehouse.

Once all bay doors were sealed, the holding area was filled with the high-expansion fire retardant foam. The foam prevented the infected from exposure to any oxygen absorption, rendering the creatures immobile and medically deceased within seven minutes. The remains, which were considered highest-level biohazardous, were bulldozed into containment cases, which were loaded into the trucks parked at the bays in the back of the building, and carted away for incineration. Since the foam and incinerated Skells were both biodegradable, it was a pretty green facility as well.

They had just received a large shipment from the Trenton area. Randy Aspiras was working in the main control center overseeing the entire operation.

"Why is camera 1 rotating?" He asked one of his techs. Camera 1 was supposed to be a stationary camera on the front of the building. It should never be moved.

"Um, I don't know, sir. I just noticed two other cameras acting erratically as well," the tech responded.

In front of them, a wall of monitors that they called the Knowledge Wall displayed over a dozen cameras that were positioned around the facility. Some of the cameras seemed to be zooming in and out, as if being focused.

"Could you please figure out what is going on with these things, we're on a tight schedule here," Aspiras requested.

The cameras showed the front bay doors opening and thousands of Skells moving from the trucks into the main warehouse floor. There must have been well over two thousand by the time the trucks emptied their loads. Men in hazmat suits were prodding any stragglers. The Skells were not aggressive, merely uncoordinated and horrific to look at. Some came to their current state by consuming MEAT, but the vast majority had been turned through attack, and their bloody and mangled bodies reflected the encounters that turned them.

The lights in the facility flickered. The electronics in the command center switched off briefly before coming back on.

"What is—"

The fax machine rang and picked up. There was a whir as paper fed through the rollers and a single-page message dropped out into the tray. It said:

Welcome to Taco Tuesday. You're the taco.

Only then did they notice that the men in hazmat suits were unsuccessfully fighting off thousands of Skells. Other monitors showed the facility hallways teaming with infected as they went from office to office finding prey. Workers were running out the front door with ragged bloody monsters hot on their tail.

47
HUNGRY AND THE HUNTED

Ronan and Majesty sat together and watched the images flash across the screen. They watched the citizens get ripped to shreds on traffic camera cams, shopping mall CCTV cameras, and hacked home security cameras.

Ronan reached over and closed the laptop lid, ceasing the video, but not the screams. The cries from terrified residents emanated from outside their apartment window, which was located above the offices of Autumn Marketing on Main Street, Red Bank, NJ. They were the first people to enter New Jersey since the quarantine. It had been a difficult journey, but luckily, they had followers all around the world and in every vocation.

They even had one that prepared the Kraken broadcast units before they were parachuted in. A thrilling ride, floating down in the Connex box, but the two of them were sure to have broken a record for the most unique mile-high club experience.

How could they miss this, sitting all the way across the country, when the action was here, in Jersey? What would be the purpose of throwing the greatest, and possibly, the last, party in the country, and not attend in person?

48
AFTER THE END

An electronic, stilted voice that sounded as if it came from some alien computer spoke to anyone listening:

Stand by for an urgent message from the state emergency broadcast network.

Stand by. Stand by.

The following is a message from the state emergency broadcast network. This is an actual emergency not a drill.

Stand by. Stand by.

A shelter-in-place order has been issued.

Stand by. Stand by.

Shelter-in-place requires all citizens in affected areas to remain inside your current location, home, work, school, store.

Stand by. Stand by.

Citizens in the affected areas are not to attempt to leave the premises until the order has been lifted. You are not to attempt to reach family or loved ones. You are not to attempt to move from one location to another. You are required to stay indoors. Lethal force may be used against those who disregard.

Stand by. Stand by.

Counties affected are:

Monmouth, Ocean and Middlesex.

Stand by. Stand by.

A live briefing by the state emergency operations center will broadcast in 15 minutes.

Stand by. Stand by.

The affected areas have been expanded to include Burlington, Camden, Atlantic Counties.

Stand by. Stand by.

The live briefing has been relocated due to safety concerns. Stand by for more information

Affected areas have been expanded to include all northern counties.

Stand by. Stand by.

The briefing has been cancelled, more information will follow.

Stand by. Stand by.

The affected areas have been expanded to include Cumberland and Cape May.

Stand by. Stand by.

Stand by.

Stand by.

Stand by.

Goodbye.

49
PEER PRESSURE

The four friends drove through the early evening, a violation of the state of emergency curfew that had been enacted across all of Delaware, but they were high school seniors and that meant breaking the rules and testing the boundaries from time to time. A six-pack of beer was being passed around between three of the four teens, not enough to really get you drunk, but enough to make you feel like a rebel.

Noel was the non-drinker. A Mormon transplant with a Christian name, she was a paradox. She did not find her new hometown a welcoming place for someone with so many social restrictions and so free from personal vice. Noel No-Fun was her name at school, and once the boys realized the pretty, friendly blonde was not a potential lay, they lost interest. As for the girls in the school, there were two types: Meat Eaters and Grass Eaters. Grass Eaters were minor sinners; drinking beer or Jell-O shots at a party, letting guys get to second base, the typical teen nonsense. The Meat Eaters were the alpha girls. Sexy outfits at parties, drinking, getting high, going all the way with boys. If Meat Eaters did not have some dirt on you, even a little dirt, Grass Eater-type dirt, then you could not be trusted in their eyes. Noel No-Fun offered them nothing to hang over her head, so she was ostracized.

Until she found Kyle.

Sitting directly behind her was her polar opposite, Michelle. Drinking warm beer that she had stolen from her stepdad's garage was not how she usually spent her nights. Michelle was in exile. She once ran with the popular girls, the coolest crew in school. She partied, she dated the most popular guys, and she was promiscuous. A bit too promiscuous. She loved being the center of attention, to have the type of power that comes when you can walk through the halls of school knowing every guy wants you and every girl wants to avoid being the subject of your insults. She had that until one of the other popular girls found a sexting exchange between her boyfriend and Michelle. The messages and photos spread through the school like a virus, and just like that, Michelle was an outcast. Friendless and alone, until she, too, found Kyle.

As Michelle gazed out the window, sipping the warm beer and wishing she was back on top of the high school power structure, she did not notice the longing gaze from Mark sitting next to her.

In another time, another place, Mark would have also been happier. Nicknamed Love, as Mark seemed to instantly fall in love with every girl he fancied, but they never reciprocated. His emotions were as raw as if his skin had been removed and his body consisted of nerve endings. He was a nice guy, so he could never break out of the "friend zone" with girls. Girls to him were like a beach ball in a pool. The more aggressively he chased the ball, the more his actions pushed the ball farther away. Now his eyes and heart were on Michelle. He was so in love with her that he felt as if his heart would explode. Mark was just too sensitive to fit in with other high school boys. He could not understand why the girls he tried to romance were only interested in dudes who treated them like shit. He just did not fit in, until he met Kyle.

Kyle was an enigma. He was handsome and athletic, but not popular. He was on the wrestling team, as wrestling was one of the few sports that did not require teamwork. He against his opponent alone. No relying on others, no false camaraderie. He preferred being alone. He didn't even socialize with the team other than practice. He felt he needed to oppose whatever was the norm. He felt no sense of ease around anyone and could not tolerate anyone's interest in topics that he did not feel were serious. He could be insufferable, even beyond that of a normal seventeen-year-old. People saw him as arrogant, aloof, and rude, but he saw himself as honest, and lacking in pretense. Both views were accurate.

He liked Noel because she held to her religious convictions, but did not try to force them on others. He liked Mark because the kid offered no challenge to Kyle's need to be in control of everyone that was within his space. He was still ambivalent about Michelle, as he could tell she was out with them because it was her only option other than sitting home with her mom and stepdad, whom she loathed. Also, her presence kept Mark focused on her and not talking all the time.

They had originally gotten together to go to a party at a classmate's house, but upon pulling up and seeing the rowdy group of teens chugging from two kegs on the back deck, they decided to leave and just hang out together. Three of them were not interested in staying, though Michelle was still very eager to be welcomed back into the collective fold.

They drove around the empty streets, listening to music, watching the night sky and the endless trees whiz by.

Noel No-Fun saw them first: two Skells up ahead, standing aimlessly on the side of the road. Kyle slowed the car down so they could get a look. It was the first time they had seen the infected in real life. They had been watching scenes of infected being rounded up on television, but so far, none had been seen in their own state. The Skells awkwardly turned and their eyes followed the slow moving car as it went past, four young faces inside staring wide-eyed at their first real zombies.

Kyle pulled the car over to the side of the road.

"Why are you stopping?" Noel asked, frightened. "Keep going!"

"No, wait, I want to see them," Michelle chimed in, relishing the chance at some excitement.

"So what do we do?" Mark asked. "Does anyone have that WALKR app on their phone? Should we report them?"

The two Skells, both men in blood-soaked suits, walked towards the stopped vehicle.

"My God, they're coming. Go," shrieked Noel, growing more panicked.

"They can't get in the car, everyone lock your doors," Michelle said with a bit of a thrill in her voice.

Mark realized he needed to man up. "Yeah, when they come close, I'll take their picture and report them."

"They're zombies, shouldn't we kill them?" Michelle asked

"No!" yelled Noel.

"Umm, I don't think that's legal. You can't just kill people," Mark said.

Michelle wanted to see if there were any real men in the car. "But they're not people, they're zombies. The news said that if you are in a life-threatening situation, you can kill the infected."

"We are not in a life-threatening situation, we need to just drive away. I want to go home," Noel said, her voice trembling.

Lights appeared behind them from another car. They must have also seen the Skells. The second car also slowed, then pulled over. There was little hesitation from the occupants. It also carried a foursome, two seniors from the school's football team and two girls from the sophomore class.

Immediately after pulling over, the two football players were out of their car, taunting the Skells, making a big show of it for the younger girls still in the car.

The two infected turned their focus from Kyle's group to the two new bodies that were more accessible. The first football player ran towards one of the Skells and gave him a hard kick. The emaciated man in the suit flew backwards to the cheers and laughter of the jocks. The two then set their attention on the remaining walker and positioned themselves on either side for a monkey in the middle session, throwing a beer can back and forth between each other seeing which could get closer to the snapping, reaching Skell.

The roof light in the car went on and everyone jumped. Kyle had opened his door and began getting out.

"Kyle, stop!" yelled Noel.

He closed the door and walked towards the Skell-bullying.

"Just leave them alone," Michelle said through the window to Kyle. She looked closer at the two jocks. "I think I hooked up with one of them once," she uttered more to herself than anyone in particular.

Mark realized this was his chance to show off for Michelle and also got out of the car.

"Idiots," Michelle said and leaned over, locking all the doors to the car.

Noel was now near tears.

One of the jocks, named Brian, saw Kyle coming over. "What's up, dude, am I being too rough on your date?"

"Why don't you guys leave that person alone?" Kyle said. Calm.

Mark fiddled with his phone. He had tried to dial 911, but was not getting through. He scrolled through the app store on his phone, trying to find the new zombie-reporting program.

"Why fucknut?" was Brian's response. "You sticking up for these things now?'

The Skell that had been kicked down the hill regained its footing and was walking back towards the assembled group.

The two younger girls yelled from the jocks' car. "Let's go!"

"Shut the fuck up!" Brian's friend Chris yelled back, now posturing for a fight with Kyle.

Brian grabbed the arm of the monkey-in-the-middle Skell as it lurched for him and swung it around towards the car containing the two young girls, causing them to shriek and jump down below the seats.

"I'm not looking for a fight." Kyle said.

"Didn't think so, pussy. The only fighting you wrestlers do is rolling around on a mat with other guys. Fucking pussy," said the jock who was running out of insults to call Kyle.

"Knock it off, Brian," said Michelle. She was out of the car and walking up to them.

"Oh, shit, how the skank has fallen. You reduced to hanging out with these losers now?" Brian said.

The Skell that had been thrown against the car was clawing at the windows, trying to get at the two screaming sophomore girls. The other jock grabbed the Skell by the back of his belt, revealing a 9-millimeter gun in a holster at the small of his back.

"Holy shit, this one's packing!" Chris yelled, pulling the gun free. He toyed with the pistol, having never held one. He pointed it in the direction of the woods and pulled the trigger, getting no reaction.

"Check the safety." Brian suggested. He had never held a gun, either, and he had no idea what the safety was, but he had heard it on enough TV shows.

Brian's pal saw a small lever above the handle and pushed it down, revealing a red dot. He again pulled the trigger and fired a round into the ground, startling everyone.

He said, "Whoa. Awesome. Dude, we are so killing these fucking zombies."

"Hey, Michelle, last chance, get in the car with us after we blow these things away, or stay with your losers."

Michelle did not respond. She had stopped moving forward and was taking hesitant steps backwards. As were Kyle and Mark.

Out of the woods, two more Skells emerged, staggering forward, their clothes hung from their emaciated frames soaked in blood.

"Oh, shit," said Brian, but his eyes should have been on the Skell he had been throwing to the ground. It had not bothered getting up this time, but crawled over and sunk its teeth into his calf. The teen yelled out in pain and surprise and slammed his other foot down on the attacker's head. He fell backwards and with legs spread wide, he offered up the Skell free access to his most sensitive of regions, and the creature lunged forward, digging his teeth in.

The shrieks were horrific.

Chris pointed the gun and began firing at his friend's attacker, but the screams from the girls in the car made him turn around to find that two more Skells had closed in. He pointed his gun at the closest and pulled the trigger, blasting half the attacker's left temple off, but leaving his snapping jaws enough intact to sink its teeth into Chris's forearm.

The two sophomore girls began locking their doors as Chris struggled to fight his way through three more Skells on him, firing the gun wildly. One bullet shattered the front windshield and another tore through the blonde sophomore's shoulder. The other girl dove to the floor beneath the steering wheel, pulled up on the emergency brake, and put the car in reverse. It began rolling backwards down the hilly road as Chris yelled for them to stop. As soon as the car was far enough away, the young girl turned on the ignition and floored it, slamming into Chris and the three Skells tearing into him. She slammed her foot on the brake and put the car in park.

She was hysterical and distracted by her young friend, who shrieked in pain and terror from the back seat—plus she just ran over her date. She could feel the men struggling beneath the floorboards of the car.

It was all too much. Her vision was reduced to a single dot, as if she were looking at the world through a mile-long black tube. She was catatonic.

A million miles away, someone was yelling for her. Yelling at her. Telling her to do something.

Something large flew past her. She looked over her right shoulder. Brian had propelled himself through the missing front window and his teeth were ripping into the bloody wound on her friend's shoulder.

There was a pop and glass sprayed in her face. She looked over and saw Noel holding the gun. She had shot out the driver's side window. Kyle reached in, unlocked the door, and pulled the girl out. Noel, having been trained to fire several types of weapons by her late father while still in Utah, fired again, hitting Brian in the head, shoulder, and twice in the lower back, which finally stopped his rampage.

Unfortunately, his victim was already deceased. With Chris and the three other Skells pinned beneath the vehicle, it was not necessary to waste any more ammo. The four took the remaining sophomore girl to their car and sped off into the darkness.

50
MISSIONARY'S REENTRY

PJ looked down at the cards on his Las Vegas blackjack table, and then looked up at the desperate faces that surrounded him. As a dealer, he made and broke people on an hourly basis. He took no pleasure in it. A job is a job. It was his calling

Every face wanted to hit 21. Every pair of eyes. Every set of lips. Every furrowed brow. They wanted 21.

A 21 ensured that their time had not been wasted. The number 21 made them feel better. Made them able to pay for the house or the car or their kid's schooling. At least that was what he wanted to believe their winnings were spent on. Not on drugs, booze, bookies, and hookers. Blood money. No. His faith and belief were still strong. The coin they acquired would be put to good use.

Black Jack. 21. A number. A simple number was the salvation they sought.

And Pope Judas was in charge of those numbers.

"House wins," he said. Showing his cards against the green felt of the table.

The other schmucks groaned. One shrieked, "Bullshit," throwing his cards down hard on the table, which resulted in the non-believer being approached by security and quickly escorted out. Apostate.

Most of those who left of their own volition—still desperate, but broken. Defeated creatures. Wilted human beings. Others stayed at the felt altar, continuing the casting of lots. Perhaps fate would smile upon them next time.

Pope Judas shrugged as though there was nothing he could do for the dopes who lost. Lost their paychecks. Their girlfriends. Their wives. Their kids. Maybe their cars or their jobs or their houses. But the ones he pitied most of all were the ones that left and never came back. For they had lost something greater than money. They lost their faith. How can a couple lost hands of cards break them so easily? Fate had put men through unspeakable horrors and yet they did not give up. These pussies fold on a 16. They will never survive the trials and tribulations that will be shambling their way. Hungry, without soul or reason. Preying on the weak like a buffet.

Pope Judas wondered: *Do these poor souls understand that there are very real nightmares running rampant? The Devil is real. He is not a liar. He promised Hell and Hell has come to Earth. To America. His minions walk the streets.*

The demon's name is Marcello and his kingdom is New Jersey.

THE MORNINGSTAR STRAIN HAS BEEN LET LOOSE—IS THERE ANY WAY TO STOP IT?

An industrial accident unleashes some of the Morningstar Strain. The

EAN 9781618686497 $16.00

doctor who discovered the strain and her assistant will have to fight their way through Sprinters and Shamblers to save themselves, the vaccine, and the base. Then they discover that it wasn't an accident at all—somebody inside the facility did it on purpose. The war with the RSA and the infected is far from over.

This is the fourth book in Z.A. Recht's The Morningstar Strain series, written by Brad Munson.

PERMUTED
PRESS

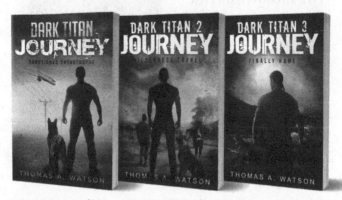

KING ARTHUR AND THE KNIGHTS OF THE ROUND TABLE HAVE BEEN REBORN TO SAVE THE WORLD FROM THE CLUTCHES OF MORGANA WHILE SHE PROPELS OUR MODERN WORLD INTO THE MIDDLE AGES.

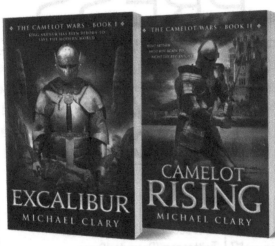

EAN 9781618685018 $15.99   **EAN** 9781682611562 $15.99

Morgana's first attack came in a red fog that wiped out all modern technology. The entire planet was pushed back into the middle ages. The world descended into chaos.

But hope is not yet lost— King Arthur, Merlin, and the Knights of the Round Table have been reborn.

PERMUTED
PRESS

PJ thought about the wretched state. The state of the state. As he did, the televisions that plastered the walls of the casino shuddered and changed from happy displays of advertisements and near-naked showgirls to an emergency broadcast.

The emergency alert notification on TV reported that the Jersey infection suppression plans had failed.

Some sort of cyber terror attack had hacked the quarantine and infection containment systems.

The details were still coming in. Nobody was supposed to panic, but things may have gone all kinds of wrong.

Pope Judas furrowed his brow.

More individuals desperate for salvation sat down at his table, but he ignored them and their lamentations. With a gentle clap of his hand, he stepped down from his vaulted dealer position, giving a nod to the pit boss that he needed to take off. He walked to the casino exit. Got in line for a taxi. Waited. Pondered.

Pondered more as the yellow cab carried him home.

His black loafers caressed the red-gold carpet of his living room floor.

Thirteen disciples greeted him, but he had no words in return. Not yet.

He undid his outfit. Stripped off his tie. His vest. His shirt. Until he stood shirtless in front of the apartment bay window. He looked out into the distance, where he could still see the lights of the Las Vegas strip.

He took a deep breath and turned to his followers. "The flock cries out for us. It is time I returned to New Jersey."